"So, you never knew your real parents."

"No. I was an orphan," Marcie responded coolly to John's discussion of her personal life.

"Poor kid," he murmured.

"Don't 'poor kid' me," Marcie snapped. "I know you read in the papers about foster homes and their troubles, but I was brought up with the greatest of care. But why am I telling you this? You don't care."

"But I do," chuckled John. "I care a great deal. I want to know everything possible about you."

"Why?" Marcie asked suspiciously. "So your grandfather can have more to hate the Waters family for?"

"Hey, don't be so defensive! I want to know for myself. My grandfather's feud has nothing to do with my life."

Marcie could think of nothing to say. She wanted to believe John—it would have been wonderful to believe him—but could she?

Emma Goldrick describes herself as a grandmother first and an author second. She was born and raised in Puerto Rico, where she met her husband, a career military man from Massachusetts. His postings took them all over the world, which often led to mishaps—such as the Christmas they arrived in Germany before their furniture. Emma uses the places she's been as backgrounds for her books, but just in case she runs short of settings, this prolific author and her husband are always making new travel plans.

Books by Emma Goldrick

HARLEQUIN ROMANCE
2661—THE ROAD
2739—THE TROUBLE WITH BRIDGES
2846—TEMPERED BY FIRE

HARLEQUIN PRESENTS
688—AND BLOW YOUR HOUSE DOWN
791—MISS MARY'S HUSBAND
825—NIGHT BELLS BLOOMING
841—RENT-A-BRIDE LTD.
866—DAUGHTER OF THE SEA
890—THE OVER-MOUNTAIN MAN
953—HIDDEN TREASURES

King of the Hill

Emma Goldrick

Harlequin Books

TORONTO • NEW YORK • LONDON
AMSTERDAM • PARIS • SYDNEY • HAMBURG
STOCKHOLM • ATHENS • TOKYO • MILAN

Original hardcover edition published in 1987
by Mills & Boon Limited

ISBN 0-373-02858-X

Harlequin Romance first edition September 1987

Printed in U.S.A.

CHAPTER ONE

SHE struggled grimly with the wheel, and pushed the old jeep far beyond the capacity of the dirt mountain road, trying to beat out of herself the long-buried resentments and terrors that had clouded her life for four months. The road twisted, and the vehicle slid in the dust at every curve. She wrestled it to a stop. The engine died. After the clamour of the machine the world fell into sudden silence, and then a family of blue jays, perched high in the birches, lectured her loud and long. The wind tugged at her long brown hair, left loose for the first time in months. She leaned back against the seat and laughed, a low full-throated chuckle; again, the first laughter in four months. Her slender frame shook with the glee of it.

'Almost hysterical, Marcie,' she told herself. The sound of her own voice brought her back to the here and now. She settled back, re-started the engine, and went on down the mountain much more sedately. The blue jays jawed at her. Perhaps that was the distraction. As she went around the next turn she tilted her head back to salute them.

In any event, she came round the sharp curve at about twenty miles an hour, and looked ahead just in time to see four men working in the middle of the road. They scattered. Her right foot jumped to the brake pedal and pushed. The old vehicle nosed into the fence-post they had just set in the middle of the road, still making a respectable ten miles an hour.

The shock threw her against the seatbelt. The jeep attempted to climb the solid cedar pole, dropped back, grunted a time or two, and stopped. This time the silence fell in on her like a great weight. And then there was a piercing whistle, like a super-sized kettle. A column of steam rose from the place where her radiator had once been, and traced a tiny white trail up into the clear Adirondack air. She rubbed the back of her neck and her spirits hit rock bottom.

'Just what do you think you're doing!' It wasn't a question. The youngest of the four men, stripped to a very muscular waist, bathed in perspiration, tugged at the half-door of the vehicle. It was jammed. 'Get out of there!' he roared. 'It could go up in smoke!'

He might as well have sounded a war-cry. All the tensions of those months boiled up in her mind. 'Arrogant damned man,' she muttered. She freed her feet from the pedal entanglement and kicked the door open with both feet, then slid out of the seat, glaring. It was not the first surprise of her day, but for one of the few times in her life she had to bend her head back to look *up* at a man!

'And just what do you think you're doing?' she roared at him. Lesser men had flinched at Marcie's roar; this one had the gall to smile. She took a deep breath and re-imposed that icy control that had made her so famous. She slid out of the car and stumbled a step or two away. He reached out to steady her. His touch was the last straw. She pulled away from him, squalling like an angry cat, her talons poised to scratch.

He raised both hands in self-defence. 'Hey,' he offered gently, '*I* didn't hit the post.'

'No, but you put it there,' she snarled. 'Why? What a stupid thing, building a fence across *my* road! And look what you've done to my——' The full enormity of what had happened began to sink in. Her only and precious transportation was sitting there mumbling to itself, with a cedar fence-post firmly embedded in its radiator. Limitless miles there were, stretching between the mountain flank and the towns of Cranberry Lake to the west, or Tupper Lake to the east—the two nearest sources of food supplies. Her larder was empty. The strange house on top of the mountain was clean but barren. Marcie turned back towards the man, glaring daggers at him. 'Why, you——' she muttered, doubling her fists at him. 'How stupid can you be, building a fence in—— Look what you've done to my car! I ought to——'

'What you ought to do is to shut up and listen for a change,' he said abruptly. He had a deep voice, gentle when *he* was gentle, rumbling like a volcano now. 'Just who are you, lady?' She could hear the miles of male condescension in his statement.

'Who am I?' she grumbled at him. 'I think under the circumstances you'd better tell me just who *you* are. It was starting to be almost a nice day until you came along, and now you've—you've spoiled everything, and wrecked my car, and——'

'That's not fair,' he snapped. Two long arms reached out and pulled her up against his hard chest, where her tears found paths through the skein of his light bronze hair. 'That's pretty cowardly,' he murmured into her wind-blown hair. 'Crying, instead of fighting back.' The words flowed right over the top of her head. Crying had been a luxury she could not afford during her forced confinement. She let it all run out now, all the pent-up emotions, all the sorrows, all the fears. There was something soothing in the tone of his voice, something comforting in the strength of him, and nothing else really mattered at that moment.

They stood there, locked together, for a matter of minutes. Feet shuffled nervously behind them. 'Can't you guys find something better to do than gawk?' he asked. Marcie lifted her head, sniffed back the last of the tears, and wiggled her way out of his grasp. The other three men were staring down the mountainside, backs turned to her, concentrating fiercely on something in the distance.

Marcie turned her back on him and used her knuckles to wipe away the tears. The old jeep had quietly expired; it sat there forlornly—looking every bit as abject as I do, she told herself. Well, I've done it before, and I'll do it now. She gave herself a mental shake, squared her shoulders, and turned around. He was standing watchfully, both hands on his hips.

'Now, you were saying why you are building a fence across my road,' she said calmly.

'Don't believe I was,' he chuckled. 'I've seen you before some place, little lady.'

'I'm not little,' she snapped. 'And I've never been there.'

'Been where?'

'Wherever it is you think you've seen me before,' she returned. 'About my road?'

'As it happens, it's my road. Right from where that fence-post stands, all the way to the bottom of the hill.'

'Mountain,' Marcie corrected automatically. 'And I happen to know that the foot of the mountain is owned by Bill Harley, and he's at least eighty years old, and you're not him.'

'Hill,' he laughed. 'It's only seven hundred fifty feet high, in the middle of the Adirondack Park that's almost flat land. And Bill is my grandfather.' He took one or two steps forward; she backed off to the edge of the road. 'So you've never been there, huh? And you're right, you certainly aren't little, lady.' He took one more step towards her. She backed up, and off the edge of the road, into the little drainage ditch. The bottom of the ditch was muddy.

'And don't be too sure about the second part either!' Marcie snarled as she fought her way up on to the road. He offered a hand, as did one of the other men. She grabbed gratefully at the older man's paw, and was restored to level ground.

'How am I going to get groceries now?' she grumbled, surveying her car again.

'Not so fast,' he chuckled. 'Holding a conversation with you is like wrestling with a greased pig! Now, you have a name of some kind?'

'Marcie,' she told him coldly. 'My friends call me Marcie. I'd rather you didn't.'

'Which leaves me with just "Hey, you"; is that what you're saying?'

'I don't really see any reason why you should be calling me anything at all,' she snapped.

'Well then, miss,' he growled, 'just what are you doing here? I would have sworn nobody was up on that hill.'

'I own it,' she grumbled. 'The top of the hill. I just learned—I—I acquired it. I drove in last night, during that thunderstorm.'

'Oh Lord,' he said, slapping his forehead with his palm. 'You mean you've bought the place already from the old codger's estate? That's what my grandfather was afraid of.'

'Well, he doesn't have to be afraid of me,' she sighed. 'I've never been here before, but I——' She clamped her lips shut. But I needed a hole to hide in, a place to get away from those newspaper men, a place to rest in, to restore my sanity. And already there are cracks in the little wall I was building for myself!

'But I what?' he prodded.

'Nothing,' sighed Marcie. Her head was becoming too heavy for her slender neck. It bowed under the weight, and the full swathe of her hair came forward to shield her face. Wearily she stepped around him and began to plod back up the hill. Behind her she could hear an outbreak of conversation. It went on until she was well out of sight, until finally the deep voice made a few statements, and quiet returned. She plodded on. The blue jays were waiting in ambush. They harried her up the road, and out on to the clearing. The sight of it restored her courage; it was so unusual. If only I could have known I had a great-uncle, she told herself. What a strange man he must have been! Uncle Jack. What a lovely sound. And I thought I hadn't a blood relative in the world.

She took deep breaths, inhaling air that might have blown all the way from Canada down into this upper section of New York state. The mountains of the Adirondack Park area were all around her, public lands to be forever wild, private enclaves to continue to exist, but under strict building and usage control. My mountain! Well, the top half is my mountain, Marcie reassured herself, regardless of who that big lout might be. And I won't let him—or anyone else— discourage me again! She walked slowly over towards the house.

The house looked like a typical mountain cabin from the front. A narrow wooden porch, unpainted; a big square cranberry-coloured door; and three large windows on either side. But its front was all that was typical. She smiled as she put her hand to the doorknob, and stopped to look around. The mountain top was perhaps eight acres in area. The eastern half showed the bare bones of the world—granite outcrops, with a bubbling spring in their middle. The water gushed out, filled a huge depression in the rock, then fell off the north side in a waterfall that caught colours from the sun as it plunged down. Five thousand gallons a day, the estate agent had told her. Enough water to wash a small town, and here it bubbled over, fell a hundred feet or so, and then wiggled down into the small lake that crouched at the foot of the mountain.

The other half of the mountain top was entirely different. A small peak of soft earth had stood here at one time. Workmen had excavated the middle of it; the old bulldozer with which they had worked still stood beside the front door. In the excavation, Uncle Jack had designed his house—a square with a central atrium—and had then covered it, all except the atrium, with the original soil. The result was an earth-house, insulated against both heat and searing cold by four feet of earth. The atrium, covered by a great dome of triple-ply thermal glass, braced by gracefully curved steel girders, provided light and ventilation. A series of rooms, doors closed, fronted on to the atrium; along the upper wall, near the ceiling, and along the baseboard, inches above the floor, small glass panels spread the light from the central room into the smaller rooms.

Marcie stumbled inside, let the door close gently behind her and looked around. Dear Uncle Jack. All those years, she thought, and I didn't even know he existed. Did he know about me? The question bounced around inside her head, and added a small touch of pain to what was already there. She wobbled down the hall towards the central atrium, one hand dragging along the wall for support and guidance.

The great central room, almost thirty feet by thirty, welcomed her. The afternoon sun poured in through the triple-layered roof. She darkened the room with the sliding curtains, then wearily made her way to the divan and fell face down on to it. And once again the tears rolled until she dozed.

The pendulum clock was striking five when she

awoke. The instrument had a doleful sound to it, as if it required all its energy to sound the hour. Marcie sat up quickly and looked around, from long habit, for the men. But of course the terrorists were thousands of miles away. All their masks and guns and anger were far behind her, she told herself. Now if only she could convince herself it was true!

She struggled to her feet. They had warned her, all the doctors, that she would re-live all the scenes of the hijacking for many a month, and for once they were right. And what you have to do, the final advice was, is to fight back. Keep busy, don't dwell too long on the past, look forward. She managed a smile for that one. Look forward. Get up and get with it, girl!

She bounced off the divan with all the resurgent strength of her twenty-two years. Bustle! Get with it! She giggled at herself as she pulled back the curtains. The room was perfect for her needs, almost as if her great-uncle had known. But of course he hadn't. Her smock hung on the antlers of a long-dead trophy. She shrugged it on and went over to the easel. The painting was almost half finished. Just to be sure she pulled out the clip sheet that had come with the contract. Book covers! What a way for a true-blue artist to make a living!

Or rather, what a wonderful way to keep eating while your talents waited to be recognised, she lectured herself. 'Pride goeth before a——' I forget, but it can't be anything nice. She slipped a practised thumb into her palette and went at the painting. As usual, she lost herself in her work, so when the voice sounded behind her she almost dropped both palette and brush. She whirled around.

'You again!' she snapped. 'I thought I'd had enough of you for a week! How dare you just walk into my—— How did you get in here? I know I locked the door!'

'Well, I did knock,' he drawled, 'but with no answer I thought I'd come on in. I had the key, and——'

'You had *what* key?' Marcie screeched at him. There it was again—that haunting feeling, that knowing that nothing she was or had was private to her. Knowing that her destiny was in other hands, out of her control. And he has a key! She shuddered, but confronted him grimly, hand outstretched. 'Give it to me!'

There was a strangely cold expression on his bronzed face as he fished in a capacious pocket, pulled out a little Yale key, and dropped it into her palm. 'Around here,' he said very quietly, 'we like neighbours to have a key. In fact, we don't go much for locking doors in the first place.'

'Well, that may be your way,' she snapped at him, 'but it's not mine. I came up here for——'

'Nice painting,' he interrupted. 'A little—sexy, but what the hell.'

'Get away from that!' she snarled, forcing herself between him and the easel. 'I'm not conducting a free show. And I don't consider us to be neighbours.'

'Well, there's nobody else living within ten miles of us,' he chuckled. 'If that doesn't make us neighbours I don't know what will. Yeah, sexy.'

'It isn't sexy,' she defended, 'it's sensuous. There's a difference.'

'Is there really?' He moved over to the room's only easy chair and slumped into it, looking as if he were thoroughly at home. He's just come from a shower, she thought. His bronze hair is all plastered down, except for those curls over both ears. And he's changed his clothes, too. Those slacks look casual, but it's expensive casual. And the Guayabera shirt—with seagulls, no less. If it weren't for those creases in his face he'd be handsome, that one. Watch your step, Marcie!

'So you were going to explain the difference between sexy and sensuous,' he probed.

She sighed impatiently. 'I certainly don't intend to do any such thing,' she returned. 'Just what is it that you want?'

'Me? Nothing at all. At least not at the moment. You gave the impression that you were out of food, so I brought you up some staples. It's all on the table in the kitchen.'

There it was again, that hint that he was not a stranger to the house. He knew where the kitchen was—she didn't. Not yet, at least. She had driven the long road up from Watertown the previous night, found the access road purely by luck, struggled up the mountain by the light of a full moon, and had dropped straight into bed. And now here he was offering food. And what else? She felt the rush of blood to her cheeks as embarrassment overcame her.

'I—I'm sorry. I didn't mean to——'

'Don't back off from it,' he chuckled. 'You *meant* to be mean, you just didn't know. I like a woman who stands up and fights for her rights. Now, what did you say your name was?'

'I didn't say, but it's Waters. Marcie Waters.'

His face seemed to turn to stone. 'Oh God,' he muttered, 'not that again!' He studied the far wall, thinking, then shrugged his shoulders. 'Bound to happen,' he grunted. 'Well, I'm not going to let that old business start again. Somewhere I've seen you before, haven't I? It'll come to me.'

'I think you're way out in left field,' her voice quavered, 'if you're intimating that I'll start some old business. You've got the wrong person. I—I thank you for the food. It will tide me over until I can figure some way to—— Thank you very much.'

'Very prim. Very nice.' Laughter edged quietly behind his every word. 'You've braided your hair—too bad. I liked it running free in the wind. As Gramps would say, you look like butter wouldn't melt in your mouth. Marcie. Short for what?'

'It isn't short for anything,' she snapped. 'It's just—it's the name I was born with.' Come on, her conscience nagged at her. He's gone out of his way to do you a neighbourly favour, and you treat him like dirt! She shrugged her shoulders at the reprimand, but knew it was true.

'Coffee,' she stammered. 'Would you like some coffee?'

'Now that's downright neighbourly,' he chuckled. 'Do you have any?'

'I—yes,' she said. 'I brought it with me. Instant decaffeinated?'

'Anything so long as it's not just hot water,' he said solemnly. He unfolded himself from the chair. 'I'll come along to the kitchen with you,' he offered.

Yes, she thought, or maybe I won't be able to find the place. She watched as he stretched upward, lifted his hands up over his head to flex them, and touched the low ceiling. 'I told Jack many a time he should have made these ceilings higher,' he said. He moved ahead of her, out of the atrium and down the corridor. The kitchen, it seemed, was at the back of the house.

'Jack?' she asked hesitantly.

'Jack Waters,' he said, turning around to stare at her. 'It's my grandfather who conducted the feud.' Again that momentary hesitation, as if he were selecting his words carefully. 'You *did* inherit this place in his will?'

'Not exactly.' Marcie was very familiar with kitchens, and for instant coffee all you needed was boiling water. She moved over to the stove, where a dusty kettle stood. It allowed her to turn her back on him, to hide her too-mobile face. She picked up the kettle, rinsed it thoroughly in cold water from the tap, and filled it.

'Not exactly?' He's like a dog worrying a bone, she sighed to herself. He hears everything—especially the things I shouldn't be saying—and he won't let go.

She carried the filled kettle back to the gas stove and turned it on.

'You need a match,' he interrupted, and furnished one. The flame sputtered, then rose.

'No, not exactly. Uncle—Jack—didn't exactly leave anything to me. He left it in trust with his lawyers, and specified that they were to hire a detective agency to find his heirs. They found me.'

'Ah.'

'Ah? What's that mean?'

'Just ah,' he said. 'I wondered why you weren't at his funeral. I made all the arrangements, and Gramps and I were the only mourners.' There was a touch of censure in his voice. 'You couldn't make it, of course?'

'Hardly,' she returned. 'First of all, I never knew I had a great-uncle, so I could hardly be concerned with his death.'

'And second? There is a second, isn't there?'

'Yes,' she giggled, almost hysterically. 'And secondly, I was tied up at the time.' It hurt to think of it. She bent over with the pain of it all. Tied up—with ropes.

'Hey.' A deep bass, soothing. No real words, just murmurs of comfort as he turned her gently round, and for the second time in one day Marcie found herself nestling against his chest, her head tucked in under his chin. One of his hands held her waist, the other patted her shoulder.

She struggled for self-control, found it, and backed

away from him. The little kettle was whistling at them. She fumbled through the cupboards and found a collection of mugs. Rinsing them off took a matter of seconds. 'Damn!' she exclaimed. 'The coffee's still in my truck, and my truck—oh, lord!'

'I brought coffee,' he assured her, reaching into one of the paper bags on the table. She accepted it, her hand shaking, and broke the seal. Her movements were automatic. Spoon coffee into the mugs, pour in the boiling water, and—'I don't have any milk,' she sighed. 'The refrigerator is——'

'It all runs on propane gas,' he told her. 'I'll turn it on for you in a few minutes, and tomorrow I'll bring up a couple of fresh tanks for you. And your jeep is being repaired. The men towed it down to Tupper Lake this noontime. The mechanic says it needs a new radiator, and they'll have it on the road in a couple of days.' He thumped down into one of the solid captain's chairs that surrounded the kitchen table. Listen to that, Marcie told herself as she slid gently into one of the others. He must weigh over two hundred pounds! And all muscles. I wonder if his head is that way too?

He sipped at the black brew and gave a sigh of contentment. She managed a tiny taste of hers. Her fingers must have slipped—the coffee was far too strong for her. She spluttered.

'Too hot?' he enquired.

'Uh! Yes,' she gabbled. 'Too—too hot.'

He slugged down another draught of the stuff. 'Just a little weak,' he offered. 'So you're a painter?'

'No, I'm an illustrator. Maybe some day I'll be a painter.' That is if the reward money held up, and living up here in the mountains was as cheap as she had anticipated. He dashed her hopes.

'Better get famous in a hurry,' he advised. 'The Adirondacks were once an ideal place to live, but now with the tourist trade, and the Olympics, and things like that, prices are sky-high.'

'Oh, my!' It was all she could think of to say. Usually voluble, Marcie had run out of words. It hardly seemed possible. He was staring at her over the lip of his mug. She could almost see the wheels turning inside his head. *I've seen this woman before!* Give him enough time and he'd remember. *Think of something, quick!*

'My great-uncle,' she stammered. 'You knew him?'

'Did I ever,' he laughed. 'He and my grandfather made some pair.'

'They were friends?'

'A long time ago they were partners in our law firm down in the City.' She knew what that meant without explanation. New York City, of course. Lawyers?

'And then?'

'And then they both decided to retire, bought up all this land, built their houses, and discovered it was more fun to fight than be friends. That's why I was building the fence.'

'I—I must be tired, or something,' she said, puzzled 'I don't understand.'

'They ended up running a grade A feud, with your uncle up on the hill, and my grandfather down in the hollow. About a woman, of course.' A distant cynical expression dashed across his face. 'If Gramps left that access road open and in use for a year and a day it would become a legal road for anyone to use. To maintain his rights, he has to close it at least once a year. So when he told me to close the road, not knowing that you were up here on the mountain already, I figured today was as good a time as any to get it done. Besides, we both figured that Jack's estate would be auctioned off, and we didn't want any prospective buyer thinking he owned a right-of-way across our property.'

'But—but how would anyone get up here?'

'The same way they've been doing for years before your uncle took it into his head to bulldoze the road. Shanks's mare, they say in these parts. There's a footpath—a small nature trail—that can be used.'

'And your grandfather and my—and Uncle Jack, they just didn't get along?'

'I guess you could say that. There was something to do with—well, I guess it must have been your mother.' Again that flinty expression showed. 'She was supposed to marry my father, and ended up marrying yours. But it was the road, really, that finally broke things up. Your uncle just ploughed ahead with his new toy, and Gramps didn't find out about it until he went into Star Lake one day and heard the scuttle-butt—the rumours. Did that ever make him mad! He sat out there in the middle of the road for two days with his shotgun in hand, daring your uncle to come down the road!'

'It—it sounds pretty silly,' remarked Marcie.

'Aren't most feuds?'

'I don't know.' But she did know, of course. That was what was behind the entire hijacking—a bitter feud between two religious sects, each trying to outdo the other in the modern world of instant communications. Two old men perched on a mountain, struggling to do just what those wild-eyed assassins had done to her and the entire plane load of passengers. She shuddered again. When she looked up he was staring at her again.

'Don't look at me like that,' she complained.

'Like what?' he chuckled. 'Sensuously?'

'Don't talk like that!' she raged. 'It's only a book cover. It's what I do for a living. Romances. They send me the cut sheets, and I do the paintings. And maybe some day, when I've really learned how to paint, I'll do something else.'

'Makes sense,' he allowed as he stood up. 'Well, I've got to get back down the hill. I'll tell Gramps about you.'

Marcie stood up with him, marvelling at the ease with which he moved. It made her feel awkward. 'Perhaps I could talk to him some day?' she suggested.

'I don't know,' he said. 'Old feuds die hard. If you're Jack's blood relative, I doubt if Gramps is willing to bury the hatchet any time soon. I'll light the refrigerator for you, and the pilot light on your stove, and be on my way.'

He did so with an economy of movement, pulling out trays she never would have expected to find, lighting the little burner that somehow transferred heat into cold, the pilot light that provided automatic ignition to the stove, and then closing it all up again. 'And that's almost that,' he said sombrely. 'I forgot something else.'

'What?'

'This.' He leaned over without putting his hands on her and kissed her gently on the lips. It was like a brush with a passing spring breeze, cool yet warm, light yet heavy, impetuous yet serious. She was still standing there as he walked out of the kitchen. 'But I sure as hell wish your name wasn't Waters,' he called back over his shoulder. Marcie shook her head in disbelief.

'Three on one match!' she marvelled. 'He lit up me and the stove and the refrigerator. Lord, what sort of a man is that?' But that's a sign of bad luck. You'd better not tangle with a man like that, Marcie, her conscience nagged. There was something strange about that kiss. It was almost as if he hated to do it, but couldn't stop himself. And he wishes your name wasn't Waters! Keep your distance. He's just another hijacker!

The thought pricked at her. She wandered back to the atrium, decided not to work any more for one day, and strolled to the front door. It was the easiest thing in the world to drag one of the old wooden rocking chairs out on to the tiny veranda. She settled into it and looked out over her new world, where blue jays nagged, water gurgled in large quantities, and huge men came by just to leave a tantalising kiss. Despite all the initial problems, it had become altogether a pleasant day.

CHAPTER TWO

THE sun sparkled through the transparent roof over the atrium and struggled in through the open door of Marcie's bedroom. She kicked off the covers and stretched luxuriously. Her back muscles ached slightly. The long spring evening had been spent in painting, finishing her cover illustration. And then exploration, raising questions for which she had no answer. Hot and cold water, for example. The cold water was evidently direct from the spring outside, chillingly cold; the hot from some mysterious source. It was there instantly when she turned on the tap, one hundred degrees or more, and plentiful. But from where? She had showered for almost half an hour on the previous night, and still it ran hot and strong!

'Which is something you'll just have to find out for yourself,' she chortled, as she swung her lithe frame out on to the warm rug. Her shortie nightgown twirled and untwisted to mid-thigh as she stopped in front of the full-length mirror. 'Not bad, little lady,' she told herself, and laughed because she had adopted *his* phrasing. Her mirror-image laughed back at her and her long mass of light brown hair swung around her like a halo. Not bad at all. A pert, well-fleshed figure; a nice smile that translated an ordinary face into beauty; and the worry lines were fading from her forehead. Worry lines. Look at you! Four weeks hidden under an ugly black chador because your captors hated to admit you were a woman. Four weeks, tied to chairs, handcuffed to a miserable bed. They had once offered to release her, but she had

22

refused to go without all sixteen of the men. And, since she was the only passenger who spoke Arabic, she had become a gadfly to the men who tried to pose as religious fanatics. They could not match her own ability to quote the Koran. She shrugged, and shook herself to break free from her reminiscences.

Breakfast was a treat. Bacon and eggs and bread, all provided by her—thoughtful—neighbour. Coffee too, for that matter, even though she would have preferred tea. She giggled as she carried her mug out of the atrium and threw back the cover over her newest painting. A very wholesome girl stared back at her. She was sharing the seat on a bulldozer with a very large, very attractive man. On a bulldozer, no less. How romantic can you get! But that was the requirement. Illustrators provided what art directors wanted.

Another day of drying, and then I've got to find a post office, she told herself. Look at that man. Not at all the man I thought of when I started the painting. In fact—oh, lord!—it's him to the eyeballs! Suppose he came up and—oh, me! Did I get those eyebrows right? If I can just smuggle it off the mountain I'll be all right. He can't possibly read romance novels, can he? There's something about the tip of the nose that I ought to touch up. Yes, her conscience nagged at her, and if you touch up everything you can think of, you'll never get it mailed. There has to be a time to stop, and this is it.

'And you're so right,' she laughed aloud. 'So right!'

'Who's so right?' Just behind her left shoulder, that deep voice, that touch of steel. She sprang forward instinctively and pulled the cloth cover down over the painting.

'You——What the devil are you doing in my house?' She raised both balled fists in front of her. He held up his hands in surrender and backed away.

'I give up,' he pleaded facetiously. 'Don't hit me, I give up!'

'And how did you get in this time?' Marcie snarled at him. 'Don't tell me you've got a collection of keys!'

'I'm afraid I can't tell you,' he chuckled, 'you told me not to. But if it makes you feel any better, you left the front door open, which is as good as an invitation around these parts. Not going to let me see the finished product?' He took a step or two towards the easel, but she flung herself in front of him.

'No. No, I'm not. No!'

'OK, I understand. One "no" would have done it. So hurry up.'

'Hurry up for what?'

'Well, you can't go fishing in *that*.' His thumb made a gesture towards her nightgown. Marcie took a deep breath to keep from exploding. The gown left litle enough to the imagination when neatly cleaned and pressed. Now, all rumpled, clinging to her in several interesting areas, it was more like a road map to seduction.

'Oh, my God,' she muttered. Her hands came up over her breasts as she backed away from him. He stood there with his hands on his hips, a wry smile playing across the furrows on his face. Three steps were enough to get running room. She turned and ran for the bedroom, slamming the door behind her. His bellow of laughter followed her, echoing through her mind as she fumbled for a light switch, and found one.

She flipped it down, and a tiny pinpoint of light appeared. Not much—perhaps as much as a couple of fairy lights on the Christmas tree—but there was plenty of light streaming in through the panels from the atrium for her to see by. She blinked as she walked over to the bureau. Inadvertently she stopped in front of the mirror.

Look at you! she swore silently. Lovely figure, nice complexion, lovely hair, and a face that looks like a Plain Jane, for sure. Going fishing? Maybe I ought to slip into a bathing suit—and a brown paper bag to go over my head? She stamped her foot, angry with herself. There were enough people in the world to tell you how homely you are, without you doing a number on yourself! All you have to do is smile a lot; you've got marvellous teeth.

Oh, cut it out, she argued with herself as she riffled through the contents of the bottom drawer. A bathing suit. There's a bikini down at the bottom of this mess of stuff. That ought to make him overlook a—— What the devil am I doing, acting as if his opinion were important? She whipped out the blue costume, and struggled into it. Tight fit, that. When she had come back from the hijacking she had been all skin and bones, and had purposefully fed herself four meals a day to make up for it, slightly overdone, perhaps?

Her mirror agreed with her. She told it emphatically to mind its own business, picked up a light sweater for her shoulders, and strolled out into the atrium as if she hadn't a care in the world. He was sprawled out on the divan, waiting. Or maybe that's wrong, she told herself. There's so much of him that it just seems as if he sprawls. And if he's looked at that painting I'll kill him.

She sidled by him cautiously, re-arranging the cloth over the easel with what she hoped looked like an idle hand. 'I'm ready,' she said cheerfully. 'But I don't understand this sudden urge to take me fishing.'

'This damned feud has been tearing my family up for years,' he said bitterly. 'It's time to put an end to it.'

'But you said it was only your grandfather,' she stammered.

'Yes. And my mother,' he returned. She could feel the hard edges around the words. 'Nobody ever thinks about my mother. When she found out——'

'Found out what?'

'When she found out she was only a second-best choice, it broke her up completely. She divorced my father soon after I was born, and took me off with her. Oh, I was raised on a dose of the wicked Waters family, three times a day. And now's the time to start breaking it up. We'll use the fishing excuse to see if I can make Gramps accept you.' He stared into space for a moment, his face a mask. And then, as if he had been away somewhere, 'The fish would admire that suit. No bikini?'

'I——No,' lied Marcie. 'I like to—no, no bikini.'

'No matter,' he chuckled. 'It's just a mite chilly in the mountains in May.'

'You think it might be too cold for just a——'

'Not too cold.' He was trying to be solemn, and not having too much success. 'The flies will love it.'

'I guess I don't know what you're talking about,' she grumbled. 'First it's cold, but not too cold, then it's flies. Just what *is* it?'

'OK, I apologise,' he rumbled. 'You look lovely in that thing.'

'You need your eyes examined,' she returned. 'The flies?'

'Yes, the flies. In the spring the black flies come home to the Adirondacks,' he told her. 'They'll eat you up, little lady. They especialy like nice well-rounded female blood. Take a look at what I'm wearing.'

Marcie did, embarrassed. She hadn't noticed what he was wearing at all. A long-sleeved shirt, with a high buttoned collar. Jeans, tucked into half-boots. A hat in

his hand, with a net suspended from its brim. Only his
face and neck were visible. She groaned.

An hour later she was scrambling down the narrow
trail on the north face of the mountain, trying her best
to keep up with him. For the swimsuit she had
substituted her only pair of tracksuit trousers. An old
long-sleeved shirt, liberally splattered with paint,
concealed her finest assets. Her face glowed with the
insect repellant he had forced on her, and one of his
old hats was clamped down on her head. Crammed, to
be truthful. All her pride and joy, her hair, was
crammed up under that miserable, hateful hat. Why
do I do it? she demanded of herself. Why? I could
have stayed in my little house on top of my little
mountain, and—look at me! Almost in tears, she
slipped on a rocky outcrop, slid merrrily down the
path on her widest proportion, gathered him up as she
knocked his legs from under him, and precipitated
them both to the very edge of the lake.

'Well, that's one way to do it,' he said solemnly as he
slid off her lap. 'I don't recommend it for everyday
work, but—— Hey, no tears! You cried on me
yesterday; that ought to be enough for a week.' Marcie
sat up, struggled to shut off the waterfall, and
knuckled her eye to brush away the penultimate tear.
He got the last one, leaning back over her to kiss it off
her cheek. She could feel the shock of it rattling off the
heels of her borrowed boots. The mere contact.

'It's the boots,' she muttered. 'They're too big.'

'Of course,' he agreed, pulling her gently to her feet.
For a moment they stood toe to toe, he holding both
her hands in his. He broke the hypnosis, dropping her
hands and turning quickly away. She watched his
back, dumbly, still shaking—from the slippery slide
down the mountain, she told herself fiercely; not from

him, from the slide! She forced herself to hobble after him.

There was a beach of sorts, and a rickety dock, with a curious boat tied up at its end. There was a cove in the mountainside, a pine-guarded enclave. Sitting up at the top of its slight slope was a log cabin of massive proportion. Smoke idled from one of its two chimneys. The front door opened, and a tall lean figure came out on to the porch and stopped.

'Hey, Gramps!' called John Harley, and waved. The old man glared at them, went back into the house, and slammed the door. John shrugged his shoulders. 'It's going to be one of those days,' he sighed.

'I'd like to meet him,' she offered hesitantly.

'When we come back,' he sighed. 'I tried to talk him into it at breakfast. He's old, Marcie. He sees what went on twenty years ago, rather than what goes on today. Come on.'

That strong hand again, sweeping hers up and towing her down the length of the dock. The structure creaked under his weight. 'Watch that hole,' he warned. 'I've got to—damn it, I just don't have the time, and getting something done up here is almost impossible. The local people would rather fish than do carpentry.'

'Even as you and I?'

He grinned at her, and helped her down into the canoe. Which wasn't, he explained. 'It's a guide-boat, specially designed for these waters. Made out of pine planking. You'll note that the stern is not pointed, like an ordinary canoe. Can you row?'

'I—I know what an oar is,' Marcie offered hesitantly.

'So take the bow,' he commanded. She made her way warily forward, stepping over the cluster of fishing poles and equipment midships. The boat rocked wildly as she moved. She grabbed for the seat ahead of her, hoping he hadn't noticed. He rowed them up the lake, around the curve that shaped it like the letter 'C', and pulled up at a marker buoy.

'Channel marker?' she asked.

'Fish marker,' he returned, brushing the flies away from his mouth. 'Pull your fly-screen down before they carry you away.'

He was a serious fisherman. She crouched down in her end of the boat, hoping that no fish would tangle with her hook. He went about the whole thing with enthusiasm, fly-casting with casual skill, and landing several good-looking trout in an hour. Good-looking trout. She knew because he told her so. *Her* wish was granted. She sat in the bottom of the boat, feeling miserable, staring at the trout as he plucked them off his hook and threw them, flapping, down in front of her. She returned the stare through the interstices of her fly-net. Stupid trout, she told herself. Look at them, flapping around. If they'd stayed at home this morning—if *I'd* stayed at home this morning—lord, what a mess! His mother hated *my* mother. And what about me? She taught him to hate the Waters family. That's something you don't overcome very quickly. They might not have known I existed, but 'the sins of the fathers'?

'Had enough? he asked finally. She turned around to stare. He was casually winding in his line, checking his gear for damage, humming a little tune under his breath.

'Yes,' she managed to squeak.

'We're lucky to catch anything,' he mused.

'How come?'

'Look at all this,' he said, waving an arm to indicate the whole lake. 'Five years ago nothing grew or swam in this lake. Nothing. Acid rain.'

Marcie nodded, trying to recall what she had casually read in the papers.

'Two hundred Adirondack lakes were totally dead,' he continued. 'And then Cornell University came in to experiment. They proved that with big enough doses of antacids the lakes could be rehabilitated. But it's difficult to find a big enough source of limestone to do the work.'

'So what did they do?'

'Well, for this lake, they got five tons of ordinary baking soda and poured it in. But that's only an experiment. Most of the other lakes are still dead. And the solution here is only temporary; acid rain is still coming down. We don't know how long it will take, but sooner or later, unless we get some control over air pollution, Spring Lake will be dead again. And that is enough lecturing for today.'

He seemed to have trouble tearing his eyes away from the expanse before him. 'Too bad you didn't catch anything,' he consoled.

'Yes,' she agreed. What would I have done with one if I had caught one? Scream, probably. The fish aren't the only stupid ones around here. I'm not an outdoor type. So why am I making all this effort to look like one? Leave me alone, John Harley. Leave me alone.

The flies followed them all the way up the lake, but instead of heading directly for the landing stage, he rowed them farther north to where, emptying into another little cove of its own, the splashing rainbow sparkle of a little river hurtled down the mountain and into the lake. He waved a hand in its general direction. 'That's your spring,' he announced. 'It's the main feeder for the lake. Without it this whole area would be practically worthless.'

'So maybe then the flies would go away,' mumbled Marcie. His hearing was very acute.

'They'll do that of their own accord, little lady. They're only a springtime phenomenon. Come June, and all this will be a perfect paradise. Unfortunately, the fish only bite when the flies bite, so a real fisherman has to make some sacrifice. I gather you're not?'

'Not what?'

'A real fisherman?'

'Not so you'd notice,' she sighed. 'I'm a city girl. I didn't know milk came from cows until I was ten or so.'

'What city?'

'Where else? New York. My foster-parents are Lebanese Arabs. Hafez worked down in the financial district, and we lived out on the Island, first at Sunnyside, and then, when he advanced in his work, to Cambria Heights.'

'Foster-parents?' he queried.

'Yes, foster-parents. I was an orphan. I never knew either my mother or my father.'

'Poor kid.'

His tone irritated her. 'Don't "poor kid" me,' she snapped. 'I know you read in the papers about foster-homes and their troubles, but those are the exceptions. There are thousands of kids like me who go to wonderful homes, are brought up with the greatest care, and——Why am I telling you this? You don't care.'

'But I do,' chuckled John Harley. 'I care a great deal. I want to know everything possible about you.'

'Why? So your grandfather can have something more to hate the Waters family for?'

'Hey, don't be so defensive! I want to know for myself. My grandfather has nothing to do with this section of my life. Shall we head home?'

He picked up the oars without waiting for an

answer, and they were back at the rickety dock before Marcie could think of something suitable to say. How about that, she kept musing over and over. He wants to know about me! If I believe him, it's wonderful; if I don't—well, I'd rather believe him. I would, really!

They came smoothly up to the dock. John vaulted out and made the craft fast, then offered her a hand. 'The fish?' she asked, gulping down the thoughts that flashed through her mind.

'Yes, hand them up.'

I don't want to touch them, she argued with herself. They're all slimy and dead. And you've cooked a hundred just like them, her conscience returned. Just because these came from the lake instead of the fish market it doesn't count for a hill of beans. Pick them up, wishy-washy! So she did, gritting her teeth as she passed each one over to him.

'Now?' He offered a hand again. She shook her head, dipping her hands over the sides in a vain attempt to scrub them clean.

'Dig deeper,' he advised. Marcie looked up at his broad grin and wished she had a big club. 'There's a sandy bottom no more than eight inches down,' he added. 'Get a handful of sand, and use it just as you would a bar of soap.'

'Yeah, sure,' she muttered, but followed his directions none the less. And this time when he offered a hand she grabbed it, and was hauled up out of the boat like a ten-pound sack of grain. It took a minute or two to catch her breath, to restore her confidence. She had always been a shy girl. Her misadventures with the hijackers had forced her into a different pattern, but the new Marcie Waters was not all that securely fixed in place. As now. She determinedly kept looking out at the lake, with her back to him.

When both his big hands touched her shoulders the

shock froze her in place. He gradually swung her around. That big grin was plastered across his face again, making him seem much younger, more boyish. 'That's no way to say thank you,' he said. 'Didn't your mother ever teach you better manners?'

The grin was infectious. A little smile worked at the corners of her mouth until she was grinning back at him. 'Oh, did she ever!' she laughed. 'Miriam—my foster-mother—she was a great believer in manners, especially for girls. My two foster-brothers got away with murder, but me, I toed the line.' She reached up and tore the fishing hat from her head, and her long hair cascaded down around her face. 'And I loved every minute of it!'

'Hey, that doesn't sound very feminist,' laughed John. 'I thought all women these days were of the modern breed.'

'Don't get your hopes up,' she returned smartly. 'I'm talking about when I was a child. When a boy was supposed to grow up strong and sturdy, and a girl was entitled to a lot of cuddling and loving. It wasn't until I was much older that I found out what a mess you men have made of our world.'

'Me and my big mouth,' he said. 'I should have left well enough alone. Ready to go home?'

'I—I couldn't even *meet* your grandfather?'

'You'd make a good lion-tamer,' he returned. 'Hold the fish and I'll go and ask.' While they were talking he had been stringing the fish on an old piece of wire. He handed it to her and ran up the stairs. She didn't have to wait for his return to find the answer.

'Hell, no!' roared the old man, making a mockery of his feeble frame. There was a mumble of conversation after that, and John came grimly out of the house.

'He said——'

'I heard him,' sighed Marcie. 'Do we have to walk

all the way back up the mountain?'

'Hill,' John corrected absentmindedly. 'No. We'll take my truck.' He led her over to the side of the house where a small four-wheel-drive truck stood. She heard the screen door of the house creak behind them as they walked away, and could feel eyes boring into her back, but nothing was going to make her turn round. Nothing. John helped her up into the cab and started the engine.

'He's a stubborn old coot,' he told her. 'But I have hopes—— He'll come around one of these days.'

'It's not important,' she told him quietly. 'I don't intend to stay here for ever—just long enough to get my life straight, and to figure out what my future should be.'

'Well, it's important to me,' he snapped. And that was the last bit of civilised conversation Marcie could pry out of him until they reached the gate in the middle of the road, halfway up the hill.

'You put in a gate,' she said, and immediately felt idiotic about the whole affair. Of course he had put in a gate. There it was in front of her nose. Closed.

'It seemed like a good compromise,' he said solemnly. 'Gramps gets his fence, and you get to come and go when you want to. Wait one.' He set the handbrake and climbed down. Marcie watched as he walked over and unlatched the gate. What a quick recovery, she told herself. When Hafez—when my foster-father got angry it lasted for forty-eight hours or more. But not my John. Dear lord, why did I say that? *My* John. He wrecked my car, made a fool out of me more than once, took me—forced me—on this idotic fishing expedition, and he's *my* John. I need to consult a psychiatrist! Wouldn't that make a grand headline in tomorrow's paper: Girl Who Faced Down Hijackers Can't Face Fish! Or words to that effect. John was back at the side of the truck, one hand holding the door open.

'You said something?' he asked.

'Who, me?' she stuttered.

'There's only two of us here.'

'It must have been the birds, or something,' she managed. He flashed that wide grin again, and climbed in. He hesitated with his hand on the brake-release, and stared at her.

'I've got the stupid notion that something's going on in that brain of yours,' he drawled.

'If it is I don't know what it can be,' she sighed. 'Why don't you drive on up the—hill?' Caught it just in time, didn't I? 'Drive on up the hill, and maybe it will all work out.' Her left hand fiddled nervously at the neck of her shirt, undoing the top two buttons. Her other hand moved to her hair, blowing free in the wind. 'I've got to get my hair cut,' she said. 'It's getting to be so long and heavy.'

'It looks nice,' he grumbled. 'I don't like girls with short hair.' What? Marcie told herself. It's my hair, and I'll do what I like with it, and my foster-mother will raise all kinds of hell about it! Girls don't get their hair cut until they get married, Miriam would yell at me. But if I feel so strongly about it, why don't I just up and tell him so, instead of whispering to myself? I don't have to convince me! On the other hand, why do I care about convincing him? It was another one of those puzzles from Pandora's box. She shut it all away, and enjoyed the scenery.

'I *do* thank you,' she told him, as he arrived at her front door. She climbed down out of the truck seat, and turned to watch him drive off. He didn't. The truck motor died as he turned the key and climbed out himself. Well, she told herself, you surely don't have to *invite* this fellow to anything, do you! Obviously he's going to stay a while.

'I thought I'd stay a while,' said John. 'There are a bunch of things that need to be checked around the house. It's been closed for three months. Walk around with me? You ought to see how things are placed.'

'I—er—well, yes,' she accepted. 'But first I have to get out of this—this outfit I'm wearing. The black flies don't bite up here, do they?'

'Never for a minute,' he assured her. 'They're not into mountain climbing.'

'Hill climbing,' she corrected, doing her best to hide the smile. 'Give me ten minutes, or—come into the atrium. I'll make you a cup of coffee, and then I can change into something more—into something different.' 'Normal' was the word she had just avoided using. To a fisherman, what she was wearing was undoubtedly normal.

He was not slow. She could see the gleam in his eyes that told her he had recognised and catalogued the omission. He followed her into the kitchen. 'I feel more at home in kitchens up here in the mountains,' he told her. Marcie was fishing for ingredients, and had her back turned, but his voice rolled over her head and enveloped her with music—and something else which she didn't want to recognise at just that moment. As soon as the kettle whistled she poured his coffee, handed him the mug, and slipped around him, heading for the bedroom.

In the soft glow of the reflected light she made a quick change from the total cover of the fishing outfit to slacks and shirt. Utilitarian, but with just a little fringe of lace around the collar and sleeves. A quick brush restored order to her hair. She tied it at the nape of her neck with a little red ribbon; no time for anything else. She turned the light switch on and off a couple of times out of curiosity. A strange thing, those lights. They seemed to be concentrated behind a curtain that hung in the middle of the bare wall. She walked over and swept the curtain aside. There, set in the wall, was a complete window, looking out into the solid hillside. The lights were on the other side of the frame, as if Uncle Jack had had some idea about—— Of course! It came to her in a flash. Something to be added, and *she* could do it! She was still giggling when she walked out to where he waited for her.

'Ready?' John set the mug down on a coaster on the table. My, how well trained we are, she thought, as she followed him out of the house. 'The water supply first,' he commanded. Marcie shrugged her shoulders as he walked off towards the spring. There didn't seem to be anything worthwhile saying. Maybe I should run around in front of him and yell, 'I don't take orders!' she thought. Wouldn't that be silly—and futile? Here's where I take a page from Miriam's book on how the subservient rule the mighty male. 'Be humble,' her foster-mother always said. 'In every little thing there is, be humble and let him have his way. But the minute something big comes up, dig in your heels, fight the bit, burn the supper! The lordly male gets the message, after a while!'

Marcie was giggling so hard when she caught up with John that he stopped and gave her a very suspicious, very cautious, look. She clasped her hands behind her back and tried to look as innocuous as possible. He grinned. 'This is the water supply for all of us.' He waved towards the bubbling spring. 'It provides all the water for your house, all the water for our house, and much of the water for the lake.'

'All that?' she said deferentially, and took her first real look. The spring was in the midle of a gigantic hollow in the granite rock. The pressure was so strong that it created a fountain in the centre of what seemed to be a huge paddling pool. Just to test the theory she slipped off her shoes and waded a few inches into it—and jumped back just as quickly, shivering. 'You could have warned me,' she grumbled. 'That water's as cold as ice!'

'Is it really?' chuckled John. 'I haven't tried jumping into it since I was ten years old. But do be careful. It's about fourteen feet deep at the centre.'

'You needn't be sarcastic' she snarled at him. The grin disappeared from his face. What an actor, she thought. Every muscle under control, right? And why am I so darned interested in his muscles? I must be working up to some sort of muscle fetish! She missed half of what he was saying, catching up with him at, 'And it all runs out down that declivity to the side, where you see the arch.'

Marcie saw the arch, a great rock construction with a massive keystone, that *had* to be man-made. 'Would you mind repeating that,' she offered hesitantly.

'I said,' he repeated, 'that this basin is almost exactly level, and the reason why the water runs down that side instead of some other is that there's a natural channel cut in that direction. Your uncle had an arch built over it. He intended to enclose the entire pool—bird droppings, you know—but it cost him a bundle to build the arch, and that discouraged him.

'I thought——' she stammered. 'I guess it's silly. I thought he built everything himself.'

'Pretty silly,' he agreed. 'Your great-uncle was a fine lawyer, and a great man in court, but all of this—he paid to have it done. Of course, back in those days the Adirondacks area was pretty depressed, and labour was cheap. Most of the neighbours thought he was crazy.'

'I thought your grandfather was the only neighbour?'

'Oh no. There must be eight or ten families living within these twenty square miles.'

'That many?' muttered Marcie, trying to avoid sarcasm, but not quite making it. John ignored the statement, if he ever heard it.

'And over here,' he went on, and was off in a mad gallop towards the back of the house. As they came round the hill she got a good look at why the water ran hot, and where the little lights came from. The back side of the mound that covered the house was packed with solar panels, facing south to where the sun spent most of its year. The hillside sparkled under glass.

'Solar power,' he explained.

'I know that,' Marcie offered with injured dignity. 'Even in the city we know solar panels. Only what I don't know——' She hesitated to ask.

'So ask,' he prodded. One of his hands reached out and trapped hers, further flustering her mind. I wish you wouldn't do that, she thought to say, but didn't. It was very comforting, and wasn't that silly? Holding hands was what you did in high school, most of the time for self-protection. So why all of a sudden did it seem so comfortable?

'I—I just wondered,' she stammered, 'how come I have hot water even when it's cloudy, or dark?'

'Oh, wow!' laughed John. 'We know all about this in the big city. Batteries, love. In the opposite corner from the kitchen you have a utility room. Some of the power from these panels is translated directly into heated water, the rest of it charges the battery pack. When there's no sun, the batteries take over. And don't start that about suppose it rains for forty days. Even on cloudy days there is *some* light getting to these panels. Any questions?'

'I guess not,' she sighed. 'How do you tell if it's not working?'

'If your hot water goes off it's not working,' he retorted. 'That ought to be simple enough.'

'Too bad I'm not a blonde,' she snapped. 'Then you could trot out a dozen more clichés and make yourself happier.'

'Hey, that's no way to talk,' he remonstrated. 'I'm not trying to run down the female of the species. I think highly of women.'

'I'll bet you do,' she grumbled, but her hand was in his again, locked comfortably. It was impossible to be all that angry with him.

'We ought to check out that bulldozer,' he offered as he tugged her around to the other side of the house. 'It hasn't been touched in months.'

'It's a funny little thing,' she replied. 'I thought all bulldozers were huge things, for——'

'It's big enough for what your uncle wanted,' chuckled John. 'I'll never understand why he decided to do that road for himself rather than have it done. I think he was attracted more by the toy—the bulldozer—than by what he wanted to do with it. Suppose I come up tomorrow and start it up, and all that?'

'That would be nice. It has a thing at both ends?'

'Oh, lord,' he laughed. 'Yes. That front thing is a bulldozer blade, for clearing roads, moving dirt, that sort of thing. The one at the back is a backhoe. You use that for digging holes.'

'Of course,' she muttered. Sure you do. Just as soon as pigs learn to fly, you do. Machinery hates me—all machinery. I hope he never finds that out! 'Why would Uncle Jack want one?'

'Outside of clearing the road, I did hear him mention something about a flower garden. He had the wild idea that he could take some of this excess earth back here, and spread it deeply enough over the rocks to make a rose bed, or something.'

'Interesting,' she commented. It was the only word she could muster; John's warm hand around hers was enough to threaten her equilibrium. And I don't know why, she screamed at herself. He's a nice man, in an obnoxious sort of way, but——

They were back at the porch. He led her up the two stairs and they both settled into rocking chairs. Marcie leaned back and absorbed the scent of pine, the chatter of a pair of chickadees, the rustle of the wind through the patch of birch trees just below the house. 'I wish I could stay here,' she murmured.

John shifted his weight. She could hear his chair creaking, but she kept her eyes on the fluff of clouds floating just over her head.

'You don't plan to stay?' He put the question casually, but when she cocked an eye in his direction, she saw that he was watching her intently, a speculative look in his eye.

'I can't,' she sighed. 'I really can't. It's a lovely house and all, but I've got just enough money for three months up here. By that time, if my painting jag hasn't paid off, it will be back to the city grind for me. It's a gamble, you know.'

'But your uncle. He had plenty of—did you talk to his lawyers about all this?'

'Of course. Nothing's settled yet. They said something about advertising for other heirs, and going into probate, and that sort of thing, but what it amounts to is that I can use the house until my money runs out. Why do you ask?'

'Oh, just curious, I guess. We'll be up here for another four weeks.'

Marcie's heart delivered two extra thumps. Only four weeks? It seemed important. Only twenty-eight days to erase his prejudices against the Waters family, and to implant——But that didn't bear thinking of.

Not just now. 'You—you can't stay either?'

He laughed, a full-throated roar that tingled. 'I do have to work for a living, little lady. I took a six-week vacation because of Gramps. He loves this area, but he can't come alone, and it's almost impossible to hire good people to stay with him. So there are four more weeks to go. We'll just have to make the most out of what we have.'

'I'd like that,' she murmured. 'The fish?'

'All yours. I can't cook fish worth a nickel. Grandfather loves it. Maybe next time we come I'll hire a cook to come with us.'

'You don't cook?'

'I'm a hell of a good lawyer,' he countered.

'I—I just happen to know a little something about cooking,' she offered tentatively. 'How about if——' She was struck by the enormity of what she was offering.

'How about what?'

She took a deep breath, and drew up her courage. 'There's plenty,' she said. 'How about if we have fish for lunch, and I'll make extra and wrap it up in aluminium foil. You can take it home with you, pop it in the oven to warm, and your grandfather will think you've learned something while you've been out!'

'Best offer I've had today,' chuckled John.

You too, Marcie, she thought. Best offer you've had this year!

CHAPTER THREE

IT was a lazy pleasant time. The underground house was cool, and light from the atrium flooded the kitchen. They worked side by side in quiet companionship, John cleaning the trout, Marcie starting the potatoes to bake and gathering the other ingredients for trout marinière. She moved slowly. Wipe the fish down carefully, that's always the first step, she thought. It had been a long time since she had worked in Miriam's kitchen, learning the easy way: by doing.

'And then my father said, if you expect to make a living by driving racing cars, you'd better plan for a number of long lean years.' John, talking lazily while his hands worked. 'I was nineteen then, but I caught on quickly. So off I went to Princeton, and then to Harvard Law School.'

'And then into the family firm?' Be liberal with salt and pepper, rubbing it in carefully with both hands.

'Not exactly; there was a detour through the Army. It was *your* family firm, too, you know.'

'That's what I find hard to believe. There I was growing up in Queens, without even knowing my uncle existed. I suppose your offices are in Manhattan?' Dip the fish in flour, covering every inch of each side. Did he clean them thoroughly?

'Yes, and in Albany.'

Check the potatoes. They're coming along. Maine potatoes, last year's crop. Miriam would have had a fit at that! Oh, well. The vegetable oil is warm enough in the deep frying pan. In the fish go—one for him, one for me, and one for his grandfather. How about that!

43

He can't stand to meet me, but maybe he can stand to eat my cooking. Men. Huh!

'That sounds pretty big—offices in Manhattan and in Albany.' Turn the heat down! Dear lord, you're supposed to *sauté* the trout, not make up a packet of fish and chips! Idiot!

'Well, we do a fair amount of business. A great deal of corporate law, you know,'

I do know? thought Marcie. I don't know from beans. Corporate law—I give up. Maybe if I'm quiet he'll explain—if he wants me to know, that is.

He did, and the explanation went over her head at thirty thousand feet as she stared at the gently sizzling fish. The batter was turning from white to a pale gold. Which means it's time to check the potatoes, she reminded herself. 'There was a fork here. Where the devil did I put it?'

'This?' John handed her the missing utensil. 'Don't know a great deal about law, I take it?'

She punctured the potato with a little more strength than necessary. You're only supposed to see if it's done, she lectured herself, not murder the poor root!

'You could say that. How are you as a painter?'

'House or picture? I'm pretty good at house painting, everything considered. But I get the message. When are you going to finish that thing on the easel?'

'As soon as I can——' No, that's not polite, and you really don't mean it, do you, girl? Marcie stabbed the potato again to relieve the frustration.

'I think it's dead—the potato, I mean. As soon as you can get rid of me?'

She stopped everything. The next words were important, and it was hard to think of two things at once. Or anything at once. 'I was going to say that.' Her most humble voice. 'But I didn't, because I didn't mean it. I tend to run off at the mouth from time to time. I like your company, and I'll finish the painting some other time. Do you like potatoes *au gratin*?'

'I'm sure I do,' John laughed. 'This is a crazy conversation. How about you?'

'How about me what?'

'Well,' he drawled, 'I've laid out all *my* life. How about you?'

'Not very interesting.' Her busy hands split the tops of the potatoes and took the meat out from the shell. There was no masher available, so she used a deep bowl and a fast-moving fork to mash everything, then added the butter, salt, pepper, and a little milk. Remember the milk, she told herself. I'm sure they don't deliver. With the mash as smooth as silk she returned it to the potato shells, sprinkled Cheddar cheese over everything, and set it back in the oven.

'There's nothing really to tell,' she said, halting her busy hands. 'I was placed in a foster-home when I was an infant, and they finally adopted me. Hafez and Miriam are Moslems, but they knew my parents were Christians, so they raised me in that faith. I can remember when I was barely old enough to read and write—we would sit around the kitchen and Hafez would read from the Koran, and Miriam would read from the Bible, and then there would be a free-for-all discussion, and heaven help the child who couldn't hold up her own side!'

'Learned a great deal, did you?'

'I guess. And then I went to art school nights, and worked at Macy's days—I was in Lingerie. Pratt Institute. You might have heard of them?'

'No, I'm afraid not, but I've heard of Macy's. I can just picture you in Lingerie. Shall I set the table?'

Smart. *I can picture you in Lingerie.* But nice. 'It'll be

ready in five minutes. I guess a lawyer wouldn't know about——'

'About the world you live in?' John interrupted. 'You're right, but I intend to catch up.' He moved towards the table with a handful of plates and cups. Marcie stopped to watch him. What a lovely idea, he means to catch up. Does that mean I'll have to study law? Well, maybe I can fake it! Darn! It was a two-handed operation, to get the potatoes out of the oven and the fish out of the pan at the same time. She struggled with the golden-brown trout first, laying them out carefully on a platter. A squeeze of lemon in the pan, and then pour the juices over the fish. Lord, thought Marcie, what a lot of things I need! I hope the jeep comes back, and I hope I can afford to pay for it! The potatoes came out of the oven just perfectly—the cheese had melted, but had not run.

'It's ready,' she announced. John came back to look.

'Appetising,' he declared.

'I—not really,' she sighed. 'It should have parsley sprinkled all over it, and there should be some green vegetables, but I just don't have anything like that, and——' Her mouth disengaged. He was paying not the least attention to the fish. Those dark blue eyes were on her, devouring her. The blush came unannounced and unwelcome.

'Appetising,' he repeated. He leaned over, shadowing her face. His lips came gently down on hers, stirring the dragon. Marcie resisted for a moment, then collapsed against him, welcoming the uproar to her senses. His arms came around to support her as hers crawled up his chest, around his neck. Those muscles again! She could feel them all, pressing against her, flattening her sensitive breasts, and then all her sensors turned themselves off. Her ears shut down; her eyes closed. Only at the focal point, her lips, was there this rioting confusion. She sipped at the nectar of him, and enjoyed. When he pushed her slightly away she felt bereft, and looked up at him with a languorous appeal.

'Come on now,' he chuckled. 'You made this marvellous lunch. Suppose we eat it before it gets cold?'

Yeah, sure, Marcie told herself. The way to a man's heart is through his stomach. The way to a girl's heart is through her lips. It didn't affect him in the slightest—not the tiniest bit—and here I am going around in circles! She shook herself, seized the fish platter grimly in both hands, and stalked over to the table; John followed bearing potatoes. She slammed her dish down; he set his gently in position, and held her chair for her. 'Hey,' he offered, it was just a kiss. You don't have to be angry with me!'

'I'm not angry,' she mumbled as she slid into her place. I'm not angry, I'm just shaken! How can he do this to me? I've been around a time or two—well, perhaps not all that much. How could he do this to me? She fumbled with knife and fork, casually removing the backbone and de-boning the fish.

'You've got some skill at that,' he said admiringly. 'I can fumble through it, but I miss half the bones!'

'Patience.' She smiled back at him. 'Women do that sort of thing in a Lebanese family. Want me to help?'

John passed his plate over without a quibble, and stared as she neatly repeated the process.

'Wonderful taste,' he commented moments later. 'Everything. Tell me more about growing up in a Lebanese family.'

'You'd love it,' she teased. 'Man is king. Woman serves.' She choked on the statement. Miriam ran her home with an iron hand, but Hafez thought he was king.

'Miss a bone, did you?'

'That's insulting,' Marcie told him, but laughter ruled her eyes. 'Girls in Lebanese families don't miss the bones. Never. Well, not after they're ten years old. Your plate's empty, and I've just begun!'

'That's because you've got a smaller mouth. Any dessert?'

'No, I—I forgot.'

'No, you didn't.' John lined up his knife and fork on either side of his plate, as if they were military sentries, and pushed back his chair. She barely had time to snatch up a napkin when he was at her side, lifting her up effortlessly, and holding her hard up against his steel frame. 'Dessert,' he said, and kissed her again with the same result.

When the attack was over Marcie leaned her head on his shoulder, panting for breath. 'I do better when I have my feet on the floor,' she half whispered. He set her down, his hands at her waist.

'You hate that?' he asked.

'Me? No. Can't you tell?'

'I thought I could,' he returned, 'but now I'm not so sure. If you can do better than that with your feet on the floor, lady, I can see I've never played in the major league.'

'I just said that,' she gasped. 'I—I'm not a professional.'

'Thank God for that,' he muttered. 'I've got to get out of here. My grandfather will be worrying about his lunch.'

She used one hand to brush the bronze hair back off his forehead. He seemed to jump at her touch, as if it really did mean something to him. 'I've never ever had *that* result,' she said softly. 'I—I'll wrap this up for your grandfather.'

'I've never had quite that response myself,' he

chuckled,' and I've been in the business man and boy for a lot longer than you have.'

'It doesn't show,' teased Marcie. 'I'm twenty-two.'

'And I'm eight years older,' he returned. 'Now, I really have to go. I'll be back up tomorrow.'

She stood at the door, dreaming, as he backed the truck round and started back down the hill. Just as he went over the crest he tooted the horn twice. She waved, and went back into the house, filled by a warm feeling she hadn't known since her foster-father cuddled her on his lap when she was four years old. Nice, she told herself, and smacked her lips as she went back to face the dishes. And she certainly didn't mean the fish.

It was a lazy afternoon, and she was already tired. The doctors had said it would be a month or more before her muscles caught up to her mind, and only two weeks had passed since that fear-fraught day in West Beirut, when freedom had finally come. So she rambled through the washing-up, left everything to dry without wiping, and strolled out to the porch and her rocking chair. The sun was high and warm. A tiny breeze ruffled the leaves of the trees below her on the mountain, and a blue jay ventured up to the house to jaw at her. Marcie sighed, took it all in, and fell asleep in the chair.

It was the new slant of the sun that woke her up. Her wristwatch said four o'clock. She stretched to get the kinks out, and rubbed the spot on the back of her neck that was stiff from sitting down. There was just enough spirit in her to do a little work. Grinning ruefully, she patted the rocking chair and went off to the atrium to do some last-minute touching-up. Until the illustration was completed and wrapped she would not feel secure. Well, at least *he* wouldn't see it, because certainly he wouldn't be reading romance novels. She hoped.

The lunch had been more than she could sustain, so for supper she made do with a bologna sandwich. As she chomped on it her mind reverted to an earlier idea. There was a blank sketch pad on the easel. Using one hand for her sandwich and the other for a charcoal pencil, she began to lay out the scene that had formed in her mind. Her hand worked busily, her mind totally engrossed, until the light failed her. She put the pencil down reluctantly, lit the kerosene lamp, and tidied up the house.

By ten o'clock she had done what a good housewife should and laughed at herself for thinking so. It had been the focus of all her training in childhood. The boys suffered under Hafez's hand, learning to be good providers, and she tagged around at Miriam's beck, in training since she was six 'to be a good wife'. Miriam's quotes, not hers. Miriam held it to be woman's greatest goal, and had been very reluctant to see her daughter become 'one of those artist types'. She had nothing against painting, of course. It was something that a good wife could do—in her spare time.

The afternoon nap had done in her urge to go to bed—that and the need to daydream. Marcie wandered back outside again, and took up guard in the rocking chair. Her foot pedalled her back and forth as her mind remembered. Recall one perfect day, in spite of the black flies, and the slimy fish, and the—lord, there was so much good, it obliterated all the bad, she thought. What a lovely man. Why does his grandfather still hate me? Still? He couldn't have known I existed before today, but still he hates me. It was a surprise to her. She had never known personal hatred—until the hijacking, that was. She mulled it over, chewed on it, savoured it, and came up with no answer at all. So I'm back to square one, she thought. I'll see what I can do to find a way through his stomach, and John's too. He's not impervious. That brought on another spasm of the giggles.

'Get to bed, Marcie,' she ordered, and stretched reluctantly before she made her way back to the bedroom. Sleep came surprisingly, stealing in through the open door on the strength of a moonbeam.

The uproar woke her up. She glanced at her wristwatch. Seven in the morning. She had never been a morning person; her bio-rhythm chart showed the weakness. Nobody except an outright heathen did anything before eight-thirty, and that only reluctantly. Marcie struggled out of bed. Whatever it was was just outside her bedroom window—except that she didn't have a window! Incensed, she staggered out to the atrium, heading for the front door, then remembered she was wearing only her nightgown and went back to pick up her robe. She belted it around her with extra vigour, trying to take out her anger on the material, with no success.

The front door latch evaded her fumbling hand. She stopped long enough to force another eye open— which made two, she hoped. The door fought against her. She kicked at it, and used one or two Arabic words generally applied only to camels. The door opened, but her big toe hurt. She staggered out on to the porch. There, coming around the house like a baby mastodon, was her bulldozer, wagging its backhoe behind it like an extra large tail.

'What do you think about that!' John sat astride the little bucket seat, grinning at her.

'I'll tell you what I think about that!' Marcie took two deep breaths in preparation.

'I can't hear you!' he yelled at her. 'The machine's a

little too noisy.' He directed the mechanical monster up to the porch, did something complicated with the levers in the cab, and the motor spat, rumbled, and came to a stop. He swung himself off and strode over towards her.

'Isn't that a beauty?' he asked casually. He was dressed for heat today. Tan shorts, a red T-shirt, and canvas shoes on his feet. And don't forget that everloving grin, Marcie lectured herself. Her hands twisted as she forced them to remain at her sides. You want this crazy man to think well of you, she went on. Don't say what you want to say!

He lazily climbed the two porch steps and looked her over. 'Hey, you don't really look pleased,' he reported. He extended one finger to tilt her chin up. The morning sun sparkled through her wild mass of hair. 'Not pleased at all,' he concluded.

He walked by her and dropped into one of the rocking chairs. A sigh of contentment floated out on the breeze. 'You don't talk in the morning?'

Marcie tugged her robe closer around her; modesty, not temperature, compelled. She plumped herself down in the other chair and glared at him. 'Nobody——' she started to say, but there was a frog in her throat. She cleared it and started again. 'Nobody drives bulldozers around at seven in the darned morning,' she announced. She was trying to present an Olympian calm, but her voice was a gravel pit. John shifted in his chair and stared at her, neglecting the glare in her eyes.

'So that's your weakness,' he chortled. 'You're not a morning person! And here all along I thought you were perfect!'

She took two more deep breaths, wishing she had a couple of aspirins and a big club. 'Any minute now I'll show you perfect.' She forced the words out one at a time, like beads on a string.

'You're angry,' he sighed. 'And here I thought you'd be all excited.'

'I am, I am,' she groaned. 'Excited about what?'

'About the bulldozer,' he returned. 'It started at first whack. You know, these diesel engines are hard to start when they've not been used for a long time, and I expected the battery would be flat as well. But instead, it started the minute I turned the key!'

'Wonderful.' It was her turn to sigh, John sat still, watching her. She tried to relax, bringing both hands up into her lap and folding them slowly and carefully. Counting to one hundred certainly wouldn't help. She stared out at the tops of the trees, outlined by the sun behind them. Very suddenly it all became funny—lord, hilarious. She started to giggle. It grew into a full-throated bellow that shook her so hard that a couple of tears slipped down her cheeks.

All he could see were the tears. 'Hey now,' he said hesitantly, 'I didn't mean—you cry very easy, don't you?' He whipped a king-sized handkerchief out from a pocket in his shorts and dabbed at her eyes. One of his fingers came too close to an eyeball, and Marcie snatched the cloth out of his hands to cover her face. It took a minute to suppress the rebellion inside her.

'I'm not crying,' she said firmly. 'I hardly ever cry!'

'Yes, I can see that.'

What a cautious tone, she thought. I'd better change the subject. 'Want a cup of coffee?' she asked

'Indeed I do,' he agreed, still staring at her. 'Those aren't tears?'

'Of course not.' She thrust his handkerchief back at him and fled for the kitchen. Behind her she heard the engine roar again as he moved the machine away from the front door. By the time he caught up with her the coffee was steaming in the mugs, and a plateful of buttered toast stood in the neutral zone between them.

John joined her at the table.

He's your guest, she warned herself. Behave! He wrapped both hands around his mug and sipped. Her hand snaked out and snatched at the top piece of toast. Her appetite was poor—he made it so—but she had to make some sort of showing. 'I don't have anything but toast,' she managed.

'I didn't come just to test the bulldozer,' he offered. 'But I suppose you knew that?'

She nodded, refusing to struggle with words until her stomach had a little something to work on.

'Well, to tell the truth, it's my grandfather.' She tendered another nod. 'He liked that trout—did he really! Ate every bit of it, scraped the plate, and then wondered how I had made such a quick improvement.'

'And you didn't have the heart to tell him?' The first piece of toast had just been washed down with a sip from the coffee mug, leaving a temporarily available larynx.

'That's right,' John admitted. 'I just knew you were a very perceptive woman.' It was time for another nod. The second piece of toast was halfway down her throat.

'So I said, "No, Gramps, I haven't been practising enough with this cooking business, but if women can do it all the time, surely a well-trained lawyer ought to be able to——" ' 'Hey, I didn't mean that as an insult. Are you choking on something?' John was around the table before she could admit or deny, pounding the middle of her back with one of those ham-hands of his. She coughed a couple of times and begged for mercy.

'I'm—I'm not insulted,' she managed. 'But my back will be broken if you keep on pounding like that!' She managed another sip of the coffee. 'Now, just tell me the bottom line of this conversation with your grandfather—never mind all the details.'

'Yes, well, the bottom line is that he expects me to do as well tonight!' John's eyes were doing a fast evasion job, staring up at the dome above the atrium.

'And so you expect me——'

'I—yes, I guess I—I guess *we* do.'

Marcie shook her head, sending her uncombed hair swirling around her face. 'This is preposterous. He won't have me in his house, but he *will* have my cooking? What am I supposed to do, operate a long-distance take-away service? Every night?'

'Well, perhaps not every night.'

'But most nights?'

'That seems to be a logical conclusion.'

'Preposterous!' she repeated. There was a long silence.

'But you *will* do it?' Hesitantly, that. More of a hopeful pleading than a question.

'Oh, brother!' John looked at her then. Look at those eyes, she thought, like a big collie, pleading for a bone. That's not fair. 'All right,' she said grumpily. 'Only there's a problem.'

'You name it and I'll solve it,' he chuckled, back on his imperial male horse again.

'Yes, well, I—— It takes a considerable amount of food to do this sort of thing, and I can't say that I could afford to—I mean, that I could hardly. Oh, darn you!'

'Fear not,' he said solemnly. 'All expenses will be borne by the management. Come on.' He unfolded himself out of his chair and reached for a hand.

'Just a darn minute!' she squeaked. 'I—I can't go any place in my nightgown. And I haven't really had breakfast, and I haven't combed my hair, or——'

John settled back in his chair. 'I thought you'd never ask,' he said. 'Breakfast. A couple of pieces of bread don't make a breakfast. Ham, eggs, bacon, that sort of thing makes a breakfast. I didn't have time to stop for a cup of coffee. I'm half starved to death.'

'I don't have the ingredients,' sighed Marcie.

'I just happened to bring them with me,' he laughed. She shook her head, but was unable to hide the quirky little smile that flirted with the corners of her mouth.

'All right,' she conceded. 'I'll make your breakfast, and while you eat I can get dressed.'

'Now surely you can eat breakfast with me?' he protested.

'Not if I want to keep wearing what clothes I've got with me,' she returned, and got up to find the pans.

An hour later they were both ready. John ushered her out to his truck, and helped her up into the seat. 'We'll pick up your car and bring it back with us,' he promised as he started the engine and bounced on down the side of the mountain.

It was a half-hour of misery, that dirt road that meandered along at the foot of innumerable hills before they reached tarmac and Route Three. On the way he pointed out a mass of blueberry bushes at the edge of a swampy area, and Marcie filed it away in her mind.

Unexpectedly, he turned right on the highway, and before she could finish her protest he explained. 'Cranberry Lake is closer, but your car's in Tupper Lake, and they've got a supermarket up there.'

His truck was not the newest in the world. Its motor chomped a path through the woodland silence, and left hardly any ear-space for conversation. So she smiled briefly at him, and watched the road swerve and turn beneath their wheels. Water appeared everywhere: little circular ponds; long eel-like lakes; sparkling creeks. An abandoned railway line, and then they turned a corner and were at the head of the lake. Some sort of exposition was taking place in the public area between the road and the lake, with dozens of cars, trucks, and farm equipment on display. Marcie would have liked to look, but John waved aside her objections and went directly to the Grand Union supermarket.

'Shop for a week's food,' he ordered grandly.

'It'll cost you a fortune,' she protested.

'It doesn't get any cheaper in small quantites.'

She was beginning to resent that lordly manner, but only slightly. Every time she worked up the nerve to protest, her conscience recalled that last long kiss, and all her protests went up in smoke. And so she shopped, for roasts, steaks, chicken parts, veal, and all the variety of vegetables and spices she could dream up. It was rather difficult. While her practical mind was computing a week's worth of meals, her dreamy mind was wishing that John would kiss her again, right in the middle of the frozen foods aisle. But he didn't.

He waited until they had cleared the check-out, deposited a tremendous amount of *his* money, and wheeled the whole thing out to his truck.

'Well, I think I've been very gentlemanly, and have waited long enough,' he said. He took the egg cartons out of her hands, swept her up, and repeated that long languorous exercise to which he had introduced her on the previous day. When he set her down she was just a little bit flustered and breathless!

'That wasn't bad, was it?' he asked the world around him.

Not half bad, Marcie told herself, but I'm darned if I'll tell *him*! He mustn't get the idea that all he has to do is lay a hand on me and I'll go up in smoke. I'm not that kind of a girl, am I? And since there was no sensible answer to that question, she looked around for another stick to beat him with.

'You broke the eggs,' she told him, as if it were a capital crime.

'Only one,' he returned, after a quick inspection. 'You can't make an omelette without breaking some eggs.'

'And what in the world does that have to do with——'

'Kissing you? Not much, but it was the only quotation I could think of at the moment. Climb up in the seat. I'll go back and get another dozen eggs, then we'll pick up your car.'

'Where in the world can I store four dozen eggs?' she called after him, but he was already halfway back to the store. Marcie shrugged her shoulders. After all, it was his money.

The garage was barely three streets away, adjacent to the Upstate Auto showrooms. To be truthful, anywhere in Tupper Lake was only three streets away from anything. John ducked into the office before she could struggle out of her seat, and, by the time she had struggled through the door, the mechanic was just shoving something into his pocket and smiling.

'What luck,' John told her as he turned around, hiding the mechanic from her. 'He had a second-hand radiator that just fitted your jeep. The whole thing only cost fifty dollars.'

'And how much for the labour,' she asked stiffly.

'That's included.'

'You've got to be kidding. There isn't a mechanic in the whole United States that doesn't charge a hundred dollars just to look.'

'Ah, but we're out in the country here,' John assured her. 'Prices are different in the country, aren't they, George?'

The mechanic sounded as if he had just swallowed his cigar, but he managed a 'Yup' and let it go at that.

So they went back to the mountain in a two-car convoy, John leading the way, Marcie fuming at the neat little ploy at the garage. 'But if he had charged you the regular price,' she scolded herself, 'you never would have been able to pay it, anyway. Besides, remember what Hafez used to say—getting a law degree is like getting a licence to steal money. He's taking advantage of me, and I might as well take advantage of him!'

Her conscience bothered her considerably, which was why his grandfather was faced with a supper that night of beef Wellington with three vegetables and a lovely sauce.

CHAPTER FOUR

MARCIE lived through the next two weeks in a sort of haze. Her world was no longer a land of sharp black and white, but rather a mix of brilliant and vivid colours whose boundaries overlapped each other in rainbow cascades. It was a dream world, and the centre of it was this new relationship between herself and John.

He came up to the house every day, usually at ten o'clock in the morning. 'You don't catch me making the same mistake twice,' he had reported on the second day. 'A man can see when he's not wanted, and seven in the morning is an undesirable time. Not so?' She had agreed.

He would stop through lunch, help her prepare supper for his grandfather, and then go down the hill, generally at about four in the afternoon. Their routine differed slightly each day but, during the part of it when the light was right in the atrium, Marcie painted while John sat down to read the daily papers which appeared from somewhere. Her cover illustration had never made it to the post office; in the excitement she hid it in the middle of a half dozen other canvases leaning against the wall behind her easel.

'That's one fine mountain scene,' he said one afternoon, coming over to stand behind her, 'but that's the third one you've done this week. You planning to accumulate a dozen mountain scenes?'

'It's been done before, huh?' She stepped back a pace to get a better view of the work, and ran squarely into his chest. His hands steadied her—at least that was the idea—although his touch was enough to disturb.

'Must be a thousand artists in these mountains in summer,' he chuckled. 'I couldn't begin to guess how many mountain scenes get painted! Yours is good, don't get me wrong, but——'

She added one more dab of umber to the corner of the work, and chewed for a moment on the end of her long brush. 'But?' she prodded.

'But——' he said slowly, as if worried about making a comment. 'But that first illustration you worked on had less sense of such detail, and more, well, feeling.'

'Different pictures, different purposes,' laughed Marcie. 'Speak freely. I'm not like most artists; I've a very thick skin. My foster-mother felt it her duty to criticise anything in which a cow didn't look like a cow. But these have a different purpose. Come and look in my bedroom.'

'Now that's an invitation I'd never turn down!' John was almost in lock-step behind her as she moved towards the bedroom door. She stopped with one hand on the knob.

'I—I don't want to give any false impressions,' she told him firmly. 'This is not some invitation to an orgy. There's only one item on view in my bedroom.'

'You?' he asked hopefully.

'No, not me,' she snapped. 'Not ever. I don't play that sort of game. There's a painting here for you to look at; nothing else.'

'Well,' said John mournfully, 'if that's what's on offer, I guess I'll have to accept. You'll pardon me if I cry a little?'

He *looked* mournful, which is some task for a man as tall and as broad as he. One giggle escaped her, and then the rest cascaded out. 'Oh, you—you jackass!' she laughed. 'That's my line—crying—not yours. And I don't want to hear a single remark about neatness, you understand?' She had both hands on her hips, trying her best to glare at him.

'Not me,' he avowed with a straight face. Marcie shrugged her shoulders, opened the door, and switched on the electrical circuit. The tiny bulbs gave enough light to see by, augmented by the glass window slots along the ceiling. John strolled by her and looked around. Her bed was unmade, and her nightgown was lying on a chair. She scrambled around him, snatched up the gown, and pulled up the top blanket. 'I don't see anything,' he reported. His cheek muscles were twitching, as if he were smothering a laugh.

'I suppose your bedroom is all neat and clean,' she snarled at him.

'It ought to be,' he returned. 'I make the bed once a week whether it needs it or not.'

'And leave your clothes strewn all over the floor?'

'Why, how did you know that?'

'I used to pick up after my brothers—my foster-brothers.'

'I understand.' One of his hands was on her shoulder. He turned her around to face him. 'You think of them all as your real family, don't you?'

'They *are* my real family. Miriam is my mother, and Hafez is my father, and——'

'Hey, I was just commenting, not making some kind of moral judgment! I'm glad you hold them in love. It shows promise.'

Marcie moved out from under the hand. 'Promise of what?' she demanded suspiciously.

'Promise for the future,' he said vaguely. 'Where's the picture?'

She grinned. The teasing had gone far enough. With one hand she swept back the curtains that concealed the false window, but now, with the mountain scene fitted into slots behind the glass, and the lights rearranged to glow on the painting, it looked, almost, as if there was a real view out of a real window. She heard him suck in his breath in surprise.

'Well,' he managed, stepping close. 'Well, I just don't know what to say, Marcie. That's the finest bit of fakery I've ever seen!'

'Fakery?' The laughter in her voice belied the words. 'I'll have you know that that's pure unadulterated talent,' she said. 'There are two holders out there, counter-balancing each other. I'm working on a night scene for the other. I call it my anti-claustrophobia treatment. I'm almost positive that this was what Uncle wanted. And if you just step back a little way——' She did; he didn't. The contact threw them both off balance. John grabbed at her, whether to help or hinder was hard to tell, and they both fell sideways on to the bed.

They were laughing as they fell, but the laughter was cut off immediately as the mattress swayed slightly under their weight and then was still. They were lying on their sides, facing each other, his arms around her, her hands pressed palm-down against his shoulders. The ambience had changed. In a moment they had gone from laughing companions to— something Marcie was unable to define. His eyes locked on to hers. She could not move her head, and her lower lip trembled.

Very slowly, very gently, John freed one of his hands and sent it wandering up into her hair. She stopped breathing, tense, as the touch stirred her. The hand ruffled the shorter hairs along the side of her head, then trailed down to her ear, where it toyed with the lobe and moved on. Her breath came out in a huge sigh as the fingers climbed to the peak of her chin and then dropped of into the valley of her throat. His eyes still pinned her down, but she could not have moved in any case. All her muscles were in violent rebellion against her mind. There was something in this insidious movement that both shocked and attracted her. It was something she should not permit, yet did not wish to stop. Little pricklings of fire disturbed her stomach.

The fingers had gone down to the open collar of her shirt, and were twisting at the buttons. Marcie sucked in her breath again, involuntarily, and gasped. The old paint-covered shirt fell open. She was wearing nothing underneath, and a coolness swept across her breasts. She stirred uneasily, but his hands locked her in place until she relaxed.

The fingers moved again, in a stately procession up the incline of her pulsing proud breast. The prickling in her stomach had been translated into riots of passionate feelings, up and down her spine, short-circuiting all the sensors in her body. The warm moving hand achieved its goal, weighing the fullness of her breast in its palm, imprisoning the erect nipple between thumb and forefinger.

He shifted her on to her back. She went without resistance, ready to scream at the joy of the assault. His head moved down, until his lips touched and controlled her nipple. But he had waited too long, or moved too slowly. Her brain had a tiny moment to assess, to measure, to remember.

'No,' she whispered half-heartedly.

'No?' John's head came up, and those dark blue eyes watched her face as a hawk might watch its prey.

It took all her resolve, but she mustered it. 'No,' she said, more firmly. He sighed. The fingers on her breast withdrew very slowly, back up the path they had made, re-buttoning as they went.

'No,' he sighed softly as the last button was

fastened, and then leaned over to kiss her forehead. Still moving slowly and gently he helped her to her feet. 'I'm sorry.'

Marcie fumbled to rearrange her clothing. 'You're apologising?'

'No,' he returned, 'I'm regretting. What made you say no?'

'I—I don't do that sort of thing,' she snapped. 'I don't have a great many possessions—only myself. And that's what I will bring to my husband, if I ever find one. Me.'

'He'll be some lucky man,' said John. He turned on his heel and walked out, picking up the foil-wrapped supper for his grandfather. 'See you tomorrow?'

He said it casually, but she could hear the question behind the words. He was not all that sure of his welcome.

'Yes,' she called after him. 'See you tomorrow.' That, and a big smile, reassured him.

The week went on in a comforting pattern, as if nothing at all had happened, but Marcie knew something *had* happened. '*He'll* be some lucky man', Not 'I'. So whatever he planned for her, it didn't include marriage. It was a struggle for her to maintain an outward calm. John shook her too much, and was himself apparently not all that affected. Despite her years of training and Miriam's constant admonishments, she hadn't really wanted him to stop. If he had challenged her 'no' just once she would never have had the strength to resist. The question that bothered her all night and all the next day was, did he know that?

It was on Monday, the beginning of the third week, that the pattern altered. She woke up early—before seven—and for reasons unknown decided to get off the mountain top. Vividly recalling the fishing expedition, she struggled into boots, slacks, a long-sleeved shirt, and insect repellant. Her jeep started instantly, which was a good augury. She threw the big straw basket into the back seat, and started downhill. The birds were conducting a mass meeting and could be heard over the sound of the motor. The birch trees, heavy with dew, leaned over the road pleasantly. Here and there, a bare-limbed oak or pine stood among the full-spread forest monarchs. Dead sentinels, she thought, and wondered why. Acid rain?

At the bottom of the hill she turned right, heading for the blueberry patch. The swamp appeared on her right, just before the dirt track that led around to John's house. She braked to a stop at the roadside. Go ahead, her conscience challenged, be a devil. Drive in and defy his grandfather! But common sense intervened. She manoeuvred the jeep as far off the road as she could, picked up her basket, and plunged down into the fringe of the swamp.

The bushes were big, beautiful, and loaded with fruit. They clung to the edge of a path between hillside and water. But the fruit was all green. She reached out to test one or two. And will you listen to the big-city girl showing off! she muttered to herself. Showing off her stupidity? She squatted back on her heels and considered. All green here, but perhaps farther on there would be some ripe ones. After all, they had blueberries on display in the A&P supermarket the day we went over to Tupper Lake, she thought. But even a city girl—A deep growl startled her.

Her head snapped up. Directly in front of her, about twenty feet away, stood a black bear, the brown patches on her muzzle sparkling as the head swung from side to side. 'Oh, my God,' Marcie muttered. Run, her logical mind screamed, but the feet would not obey. She stood there, shaking, unable to make her body move, unable to think clearly. The bear growled

again, and padded one threatening step forward. As
fast as she could, Marcie rumbled through all the
prayers, Christian and Moslem, that her petrifed
mind could recall. The bear growled again and moved
forward one more pace.

From somewhere behind her Marcie heard an
engine grumble and come to a stop. The bear's head
swung from side to side again, and a patch of saliva
dripped through those huge teeth.

'Marcie!' If that were her guardian angel calling, he
had a deep voice. She managed to get one foot to move
one step away. The voice called behind her again. She
took one more step backward. The bear took one more
step forward, raised up on its hind legs, and growled
again. The sound broke her paralysis. Marcie
screamed madly, turned, and ran, losing her basket as
she went. Not ten steps away she came around the
edge of a bush and ran straight into John's arms.

'Hey!' he comforted. 'Come on now, there's no need
for such a fright.'

'A—a——' She just could not get it out. He pushed
her back the way she had come, around the bush. The
bear was still there.

'Oh,' he said casually. 'A bear?' The animal looked
at them both, growled, took three charging steps in
their direction, halted, and went off at a tangent into
the bushes. All of this Marcie had missed. Her head
was buried in John's shirt, and she had no intention of
coming out—certainly not in *this* world.

'Hey!' he repeated. She shivered and burrowed
deeper. He squeezed her tight. The pressure was
warming, comforting, and she managed to get a grip
on herself.

'Is that all you've got to say?' she complained.
'We're about to—to die, and all you can say is "Hey".'

'Well, the least we can do is go with dignity,' he told her.

He can't be that cool, she told herself. Nobody could be! She prised her head loose from his chest and managed a quick look behind her. 'Where did he go?' she asked faintly.

'Where did who go?'

'The bear!' she shouted at him. 'Darn you! Why do you do this to me? Where did the bear go!'

'She,' he said softly. 'The bear was a she.'

'I don't care what her sex is,' she told him fiercely. 'I'm just worried about her size. All I want to know now is, has she gone?'

John turned her around so that her back was on his chest, and she could see where she had been. 'Yes,' he said calmly, 'she's gone. Now do you suppose you could calm down and tell me what was going on?'

'How did you know I was here?' He shook his head and sighed.

'Woman! You have a very distinctive jeep. You parked it by the side of the road. I deduced that you were in the swamp for some reason——'

'Berries,' she interrupted. 'I wanted some berries.'

'Berries? At this time of year? I'll just bet you found a lot of them, didn't you.'

'There's no need to mock,' she retorted angrily. 'Is that how you lawyers think? You saw my jeep and you deduced?'

'That's exactly the way,' he said solemnly. 'Want some help?'

'I—I'm not sure. Why—what do you suppose the bear was doing here?'

'Looking for berries?' he chuckled. 'Hey, I don't want you to think that all bears are like that one. If it had been earlier in the year, cubbing season, or if it had been an old one, things might have been different.

The mountains are full of bears, but they're not as aggressive as they once were. There are so many garbage heaps in the Adirondacks now, and the animals prefer them to scavenging wild. There's plenty for all. But you *were* lucky, and don't you forget that. Now, shall we head back home?'

Marcie nodded, made docile by her first close encounter with nature. John found her basket and picked it up, then led her out of the swamp, up the slight embankment, and into her jeep. 'Go ahead,' he advised. 'I'll follow on.'

Marcie made the trip back up the mountain at very slow speed indeed. Her mind was still whirling; the adventure was still too close, and it added a new dimension to her life: she was not alone in this wilderness. There were still animals to be reckoned with! She managed to settle her stomach by the time the house was in sight, and a quick cup of coffee in the kitchen added another familiar safeguard.

She watched him over the lip of her mug. There was something subtly different about him this morning. What? Her mind categorised. He's earlier than usual. Nicely shaved, hair combed carefully, and dressed in designer jeans and a polo shirt, with that darn alligator on the pocket. Something about his eyes. What? Her diagnosis failed her. So challenge him, her mind commanded.

'You're earlier than usual,' she prodded.

'Yes,' he returned. He was revolving his mug slowly between his hands, as if he were sharing the warmth. But this is almost June, she thought. Nobody gets cold hands in the late springtime. She tried again.

'The flies didn't bother me this morning.' There was a question mark in her voice.

'No,' he returned. A pause, as if that was all there was to say. He looked up into her stormy face, and read the signals. 'They start to fade away as we get towards June. I wouldn't be surprised if the lake weren't clear of them entirely in a day or two, then you can go boating, swimming, anything.'

'With your grandfather sitting like Moses on his porch? I'd be afraid he'd throw the Tablets at me!'

'I doubt it. He's cooled down considerably. Say, what I wanted to ask, Marcie, is could you increase the size of the suppers for us? Enough to feed one more person?'

'It can be done, but I'll have to go shopping more often. Somebody else came?'

'Yes, a cousin—well, sort of a cousin. Grandfather's favourite. Plans to spend a week or two with us.'

'I see. Does he have a big appetite?'

'Well—I don't rightly know. He's a she.'

'Oh.' What else can you say? she lectured herself. He has relatives; some of them are bound to be female. So a dear friend of his grandfather's has appeared on the scene, and she can't cook either? It was intriguing. Some dear old lady, and—— It was worth the question.

'No,' admitted John, 'she can't cook either. I know that must sound strange to *you*, Marcie, but there it is. She's a lawyer too. I don't know how any of us got through law school without starving to death! I ate a lot of peanut butter sandwiches, myself. How about it?'

So I'll reason it all out logically, she told herself. Just the way he does. There's another mouth to be fed. Some kindly little old lady, a relative, and dear to his grandfather. So what's the rub? 'I don't see why not,' she said cheerfully. An answering smile spread across John's face.

'I knew I could count on you,' he said. 'Well, I've got to get back down the hill. I'll come back up this afternoon and pick up the food. OK?'

'Of course it's OK. I'm sorry my blueberry expedition fell through. I wanted to surprise your grandfather with a nice pie.'

'Well, in a way you're fortunate, Gramps is a diabetic. He has a terrible problem—he has a tremendous sweet tooth and can't eat sweets.' Marcie shook her head, a plan already half formed in the back of her mind.

'Four o'clock be OK to pick up the food?'

Her spirits fell several inches. Four o'clock? She desperately wanted those quiet shared hours. But not today? It was almost too much to be borne, but she had to bear it. He had no commitment to her; with guests at home he was bound to be needed there, at least on this first day. Perhaps tomorrow things might be restored to their old pattern.

'Whatever you say, John.'

'You are some kind of angel,' he chuckled. He unfolded himself from the chair, gave her a brief peck on the cheek, and rattled out of the front door. Marcie followed along behind him, one hand on her cheek where his lips had rested. As he gunned his truck in a tyre-squealing U-turn she leaned against the panelling of the front door, unwilling to lose a second of the time she might see him. When only dust clouds remained she went back to the kitchen, slumped into a chair, and wished that time could be turned back far enough to get a new and different start on the day.

Lunch. The menu for the Harley family, including its elderly female member, was to be Southern fried chicken. But that could wait until later. And for herself—a little gall and wormwood, as Miriam always said—a peanut butter sandwich. With jelly it might have been palatable; without, it was too dry and crunchy. She finished it only because *he* had said he ate it in his college years. Totally dissatisfied with the tenor of the day, Marcie neglected the easel and went outside to look around the house.

The bubbling, wrangling spring was her first attraction. It was warm out on the rock facing, with no trees or shrubs to distract, and the water looked so attractive. She dabbled her feet around the edges of the mammoth pool, a good three hundred metres from edge to edge. The cool water refreshed her. With no one sharing her mountain top, Marcie casually stripped and waded a little deeper. The arch covering the outflow caught her attention, and she moved closer, fighting the tug of the powerful stream. Strange. She could think of no reason why her uncle would have built such a thing, but then neither could she think why he would have built such a house. 'What sensible woman ever understands men?' Another of her foster-mother's quotations.

The glare of the sun was beginning to bother her. Throwing discretion to the winds, she turned her back on the arch, poised herself with hands over head, and plunged down into the chilling water. The natural currents of the pool were all against her, and she was a poor swimmer. She steered carefully away from the whirlpool centre and found relief in the comparative backwaters of the other side. A full half-hour later, tired and becoming chilled, she felt eyes staring at her. She ducked under, remembering that she was swimming nude. When she came up again she was close to the edge, but allowed only her head to protrude. Directly across the pool two white-tailed deer were watching her with proud sad eyes. They made not a move as she waded out of the pool, laughing; only their heads turned to follow her as she scooped up her clothing and dashed for the house.

At two o'clock she filled the deep fryer with

vegetable oil, prepared a spicy batter of her own concoction, and prepared the chicken. Her ingenuity had run out where vegetables came to be considered. Out of the freezer compartment of the refrigerator she pulled a frozen package of mixed vegetables, and set them to defrost. All of which proved to be a blessing. At two-fifteen a loaded truck struggled up the hill, and three weary men stood at her door.

'Waters?' the oldest of them asked. He had a fist full of papers and a clipboard, which made him the leader. Marcie giggled at her own private conclusion, but kept the screen door latched, and offered a non-committal 'Yes?'

'Sears,' he said. 'We have the freezer, the extra refrigerator, and four propane tanks to hook up.'

'You do?' Silly conversation number fifty-nine. This darn mountain seems to generate silly conversations, she told herself. 'That's nice.' A moment of silence.

'We have to deliver this stuff.'

'You do? I didn't order it.'

'It says here on the paper, Waters, Spring Mountain.'

'Yes, that's right,' she agreed.

'Then this is the place. Is there a back door?'

'No. The only other door is a roof hatch fire escape.'

'Look, lady, it says right here on the paper. Ordered for Miss Marcie Waters—by—I can't hardly read the signature.' He held it up to the wire mesh for her inspection. *John Harley*. An indeterminate scribble.

'He should have been a doctor,' she sighed, unlocking the door. 'Bring it in. Put it in the kitchen— I don't know where. The tanks go out back.'

It required four trips, during which her easel was knocked over twice, the atrium rug was scuffed with dirt, and practically everything in the kitchen had to be rearranged. 'Smells nice,' the youngest of the trio commented. 'Chicken?'

'Yes, fried chicken,' she admitted.

'It's a long trip from Lake Placid,' he prompted.

'I'll bet it is,' she returned.

'Well, that's the last of the hook-up.' The foreman had just come back inside. 'There's four tanks on line out there, and two for spare. All you need to do is turn the handle on the feeder lines. Once a week we'll send a man by to check it out. Let me light these things now.'

'I surely admire fried chicken,' added the younger man.

'Don't really object to it myself,' the foreman commented as he stood up. 'You should let the freezer alone for about four hours. That's what it takes to get really cold. You do all your own cooking?'

That was more than Marcie's Lebanese hospitality could stand. 'Yes,' she chuckled wryly. 'Why don't you help yourselves?'

Which was why, at four o'clock, she was once again bent over the fryer doing the second batch of chicken, and giving thanks that she had defrosted the entire package when she did. She had just wrapped everything in paper towels to soak up any excess oil when she heard the car outside.

'Oh, lord,' she wailed, 'look at me!' After her swim she had thrown on her painting clothes, and had done nothing for her hair. It hung down around her, still slightly damp, in rampant disorder. Just once, she promised herself, he would arrive when she looked—well, nicer. Just once!

She dived for the bathroom and slammed the door behind her. It was impossible to use her hairdrier; the tiny electrical current in the house wires would not support such a thing. Do they make a propane drier?

she wondered as she snatched up a bath towel and began a vigorous massage. The front door banged against its stop, and she could hear footsteps in the corridor. Marcie leaned over to lock the bathroom door. There was no lock. Back to the massaging.

'Marcie?' Maybe he'll go back outside if I'm quiet, she thought, and huddled back in a corner. Another hangover from her childhood. Little girls were only quiet when compelled to stand in corners for disciplinary reasons. Strangely, she felt like a *very* little girl. 'Marcie?' Farther away. 'She must be outside some place,' he shouted. So someone else had come with him. His grandfather? What a laugh!

Her hands had been as busy as her mind. Her hair, while not exactly dry, could be manipulated. She picked up a brush and had a go at it. Nothing much—just your routine combat with snarls, and then a quick tie into a ponytail. Her shirt? Nothing could be done about her dingy jeans, but the shirt——

She eased her way out of the bathroom and did a quick slide two doors down to her bedroom. At least she had a feminine blouse, off-white, buttoned down the front with pearl buttons, a little lace collar. She made the change.

'Marcie!' A more determined summons. He's losing his temper?

'Here,' she called. 'I'm coming!'

'And it's about time.' John met her right outside her bedroom door, picked her up off her feet, and surrounded her with one of those masterful kisses that she had come to love. Total immersion, like being baptised in one of those churches that insist on dunking you in the river! And I've only known him for three weeks, she thought.

'Don't have time for another,' he chuckled as he set her down. 'There's someone here I want you to meet.'

I'll bet there is, she sighed to herself. I really *would* like another. But I seem to get contradictory reports from my senses when you're around, John Harley. Why don't you go away and leave me alone for a moment? I need to stop and figure out what's going on in my world!

Much to her disgust, that was just what he did. He made off in that deceptive long-legged lope that carried him out of the house before she could settle on her next word or two. She followed slowly, not prepared to charge into a meeting with somebody else at this stage of the game. What a lovely man! she thought. I know that isn't a term he would like, but that's what he is. I wonder who he's talking to?

She drifted slowly out to the front of the house, just inside the door, and stopped. A lovely little red convertible was nosed up to the house and seated in it was a tiny blonde female talking to *her* John. The nerve of the woman! That little flick from the whip of jealousy was enough to make even Marcie laugh. Good heavens, you don't *own* the man, her conscience told her. Shut up, she returned. I've gone beyond the window-shopping stage. She pushed the door open, and the pair of them stopped talking to look at her.

The closer she got to the car, the lower her confidence sank. The little blonde bundle was tiny—true—but also a collection of some of the finest female architecture Marcie had ever seen, both on or off the movie screen. And she was standing there now by the car, looking up helplessly into John's face. As Marcie watched, the woman extended both hands, and John welcomed them with his. He seemed to be mesmerised, like a cobra being stared down by a mongoose.

Very suddenly Marcie felt awkward. It was her normal reaction in the face of 'cute' females. A feeling of guilt, as if her excessive height was a crime for which she bore a personal responsibility. And now John was gently leading the woman over to where she stood.

'Well, here she is, Marcie,' he said, stepping aside.

'Yes,' she whispered. She looked up at him expectantly.

'My cousin,' he prompted, 'Beth Fortin.'

'Elizabeth,' the blonde corrected. 'Haven't I seen you somewhere before?'

CHAPTER FIVE

MARCIE was still steaming when the pair of them drove off down the mountain in that saucy little convertible. Ten minutes—that had been all the time required to reduce her to a state of gibbering idiocy. With a few well-chosen phrases, and a down-tilt of her royal nose, Elizabeth Fortin had classified Marcie as an itinerant cook, and John had accepted it. She trembled to think what she would like to do to that man! Not only did he allow his 'cousin' to run rough-shod over the enterprise, but, after he had carried the dinner foils out to the car, he had come back to escort Her Royal Nuisance out, as if the woman couldn't possibly find her way over that distance.

And then, in a display of colossal arrogance, he had come back in one more time and tried to kiss Marcie! She barely fought him off. 'Hey,' he complained, 'what's all this?'

'All this is that the *cook* doesn't care to be manhandled,' she snapped. 'I would think one woman at a time would be enough, even for a man like you!'

'Brrr!' he chuckled. 'I didn't know winter had come back so quickly. Want to go fishing tomorrow?'

'Me?' she retorted. What's the matter? Isn't Lady Bountiful willing to go out and wrestle with the flies?'

'They're practically all gone,' he coaxed, 'and you can't sit up here on top of your hill——'

'Mountain,' she interrupted.

'OK, on your mountain and watch the sunsets. You have riparian rights on that lake, you know.'

'I have what?'

78

'Riparian rights. The right to free passage and use of the lake and all its shores.'

'Well, I'm glad to hear that. But you surely wouldn't want your *cook* to be sharing the water with the family?'

'Marcie, you are an unadulterated snob, aren't you?' he laughed.

'Oh, go away and leave me alone!' She turned her back on him to hide the forming tears. John's hand rested on her shoulder and squeezed gently. 'You mustn't take everything Beth says to heart,' he offered. 'She's a career woman with big ambitions.'

'I can see that.' And one of her ambitions is you, you—darn man! How can it be that I could have come to this much wilderness and solitude to find a man—and somebody else already owns him? How could it be?

He squeezed her shoulder again and then she heard him stomp down the hall and out of the door. Marcie followed, just in time to see his 'cousin' smother him with a predatory kiss of her own. He laughed as he drove them away.

Marcie banged her way back into the atrium, kicked a couple of floor cushions out of her way, and glared at the unfinished painting on the easel. Not an illustration, this one, but an attempt to convey her feelings about the mountains. It was one of her first attempts in acrylics, and it gleamed with light. Her hand formed around brush and palette, and her fingers began her typical small brush-strokes, as her mind wrestled with the problem.

Of course it really isn't a problem, she started out. I've only known the man for two—well, three weeks and a day. You can hardly expect to build a relationship in three weeks, can you, girl? That dull thud is my heart objecting, she lectured herself. Of course you can build a relationship—in one day, for that matter. Who says you have to grow up with some boy before you can love enough to—to what, Marcie Waters? To climb into his bed? He hasn't said one word about love or marriage or happy ever after. Not a word. 'Damn!'

The word spat out and rattled around the room. Something that women never do, Miriam had insisted. No cursing. Oh, a mild 'darn' might be acceptable, but that was the limit. Damn!

Look what he's done to me in three short weeks. I'm going around worrying about him hearing me curse. I spend half my day working up some succulent meal for him and his grandfather. Every time I wake up in the morning I'm thinking of him. All day long he haunts me. And here I am standing around with a brush in my hand while he's cavorting down there with that floozy! Well, maybe she's not. Wouldn't it be a darn sight more painful if Beth turned out to be a nice girl? Someone I really could appreciate. Wouldn't that be torture?

The third 'damn' of the day burst out. Not because of John, or Beth, but rather because poor stupid clumsy Marcie had just tipped the palette too far, and it slipped from her clutch, upside down, of course, all over the rug. She dropped the brush and reached for the palette, managing to smear a little more paint around before she picked it up. And what do you use to clean acrylic paint off a rug? Her mind turned over at high speed. Acrylics are soluble in water, until they harden! Quick, like a bunny!

She took one or two steps towards the kitchen, and her eye fell accidentally on the painting on the easel. All the light, all the brightness, was gone. Heavy dark greens, threatening browns and blacks—the mountains glared back at her. 'Oh, my God!' she whimpered, and ran for a water bucket.

Two hours later, her knees complaining from the scrubbing of the carpet, she threw herself down into a chair and nibbled on a carrot stick. Down the hill—mountain—the three of them would be dining on Marcie's best Southern fried chicken. *And me, I don't have the appetite to fix anything. What you need, Marcie girl, is some physical exercise out in the fresh air. Chopping wood? I don't think I own an axe, and I don't have anywhere to burn it. So? How about the flower garden that Uncle Jack planned?*

It was a bitterly triumphant smile she wore as she stalked out of the house and around to the side. The two deer were still on the top of the mountain, browsing under the stand of birch trees behind the house. Marcie stared at the mound of dirt that was both mountain-top and house-roof. There seemed to be a considerable segment directly in front of her, a shallow upward slope, that might very well be spared. And the tiny bulldozer stood at hand.

She walked over to the mechanical earthmover and looked inside the cab. One bucket seat stood on a swivel. Facing forward, it looked out over the front where the bulldozer blade was attached. The seat swivelled completely around, and there was a second set of control levers for the backhoe. And it started so easily. Well, at least, that was what John had said. And he had run a power line out from the house batteries for several days, 'to give it a trickle charge,' he had said. Whatever that meant.

Warily, Marcie hauled herself up into the seat. Facing frontward, there were two levers on the right, and two on the left. She tried to move them experimentally, but they refused to budge. Her feet fell almost naturally on the two pedals, much like those in her car. The dashboard contained four meters and she hadn't the slightest idea what they signified, but directly in the middle was a key dangling in what had to be the ignition. And that I can recognise, she crowed in delight. She adjusted herself to the seat, squirming a little because it was a bit high. Then one hand went out, the key turned, the engine protested, and roared into life.

'I did it!' she yelled at the mountains. The diesel engine rumbled, groaned, and settled down in a throaty roar. 'Now what?' she asked. Neither machine nor mountains offered any suggestions. Marcie licked her lips and reached for the lever on the far let. The motor grumbled, the machine swayed in place, and the bulldozer blade began to rise up in front of her. Hastily she pushed the lever the other way, and the blade went back down.

Her hand moved to the lever on the far right. It refused to budge. Cautiously she pushed down on her left foot, the one that would, in a car, control the clutch. At her next try the lever moved easily forward, and the machine staggered a foot or two forward, and then the engine stalled.

Reason, she muttered at herself. Think! The right-hand pedal must be the fuel control, with no fuel, it stalled. And all you have to do is test it by doing it again. Her hand moved forward towards the key, and then halted. She looked around the magnificent skyline, where the sun was touching the western treetops. 'Try it again,' she said wryly. 'Tomorrow maybe.'

She switched of the key and climbed down. The motor noises had murdered all the sounds of nature, and frightened the two deer away. Now the noises of the mountains were coming back to their rightful place, and she felt just a tinge of regret about the deer. She strolled over towards the spring and sat down on the wide rocks of the natural edging. The water bubbled happily, spraying her with a cool gentle touch. She leaned back against the base of the arch and let what sun was left reflect off her mobile face. It was hard to be angry in the face of a world of peace. She let it sink in, absorbing the sounds of the birds, the heavy smell of pine, the little cotton fluffs of cloud that were making their way towards Lake George.

'Life's too good to be mocked,' she sighed. After a moment, deep inside her, the voice of her conscience said reluctantly, 'Maybe.' She sat there contemplatively, until the sun had gone and the first evening stars peeped down at her, at which point she got up slowly, stretched, and made her way inside for showers and bed. And strangely enough, she dreamed of nothing at all.

Things seemed different the next morning. The sky was covered with thin layers of clouds through which the sun peeped only momentarily, and there was a hush over all the woodlands, as if all the denizens were preparing for a storm. Marcie finished her chores and then slipped into her swimsuit and went out to the spring: another quickly established routine. Despite the temperature of the water she was finding that an early plunge really woke her up, started the blood pumping. She was sitting on the edge of the spring, rough-drying her hair, when she heard the car come up. The driver spotted her, and wheeled the red convertible in her direction. The brakes squealed, the back wheels spat out a handful of gravel, and Elizabeth Fortin was staring up at her.

They stared at each other silently. Then, forced to do something, Marcie said, 'Good morning.'

'Is it?' The bland statement caused Marcie's hackles to rise. Obviously this wasn't to be a social call. She stood there by the car and waited.

'That dinner wasn't worth much.' The blonde threw down the gauntlet. Marcie was fully prepared to pick it up.

'It was worth the price I was paid,' she returned coolly.

Beth opened the door and swung her legs out. No adult woman wearing a dress can look demure climbing out of a bucket seat, but this one had evidently practised a great deal. 'And just what is that supposed to mean?'

'Anything you want it to,' Marcie said wryly. 'I prepare the meals as a favour, nothing more. I'm sorry you didn't like it.'

'No, I didn't. Not at all. Fried foods just aren't good for the figure. Look at you!'

Marcie did, and had to admit she didn't like what she saw. Not that she was overweight by any means, but still there was that excess, that plumpness that John had noticed early on. Still, there are things you can accept as criticism from your friends, and it was plain that Beth did not mean to fall into that category.

'So I thought I would help out,' the blonde continued. She leaned back into the car, flipped open the glove compartment, and retrieved a notebook. 'Here's a complete set of menus, enough to cover the two remaining weeks we'll be spending up in this lost land.' She held them out, but Marcie studiously avoided accepting them.

'You don't care for the wild country?' she queried.

'Who could?' Beth snapped. 'Well, take these things. I went to a great deal of trouble to compile them.'

'I'm sure you did,' Marcie returned. Her voice was smooth as silk. It was her 'trouble' voice, but little Miss Fortin was not at all experienced with the Habibs of this world.

The extended hand gradually fell to Beth's side, to be replaced by a puzzled look. 'Now what are you trying to tell me?'

By this time Marcie was hard at work, drying her hair in the towel she wore as a turban. 'I think,' she said very slowly, 'that the emergency is over down at the Harley cabin. Wouldn't you say? You're in residence, and you have all the necessary menus. It would seem to me that the food would be warmer, taste better and be more healthy, if you were to prepare it in the kitchen down there.'

'Me?' It was hard to tell whether it was wrath or fear that underlined the words. 'I—I don't have the time to be a damn *cook*! I'm a lawyer!'

'Ah, but you can't practise law up here,' chuckled Marcie, 'so you might just as well practise cooking! You *can* cook, can't you?'

'Why, of course!' the blonde snarled at her. 'That's so simple, any idiot can do it!' Her temper was rising, and that caused Marcie to calm down. There really was a basis of humour in all this, she told herself. Any idiot can do it—meaning me, of course. Maybe she's right. Hey, if I were all that brainy maybe I'd be a lawyer too? But just think, the May Queen here will be down there in the kitchen this afternoon, trying to make do, and she'll produce a marvellous meal, and John will sit down to it and suddenly discover what he's been missing, and he'll ask her to marry him, and——Good lord, what have I done!

'Thought of something else, have you?' asked Beth.

'Yes,' Marcie laughed. 'I forgot all my good manners. Would you like to come in for a cup of coffee?'

'I've always wanted to see the inside of this house,' Beth returned. 'Your great-uncle was a—perhaps the word is "recluse"?'

'I don't know,' said Marcie, leading the way over to the front door. 'I never knew him.'

'Oh?' The glint of surprise was quickly covered over. They trailed out to the atrium. 'You paint?'

'In a manner of speaking,' Marcie acknowledged. The thunderously dark painting still sat on the easel. 'Why don't you sit down, and I'll bring the coffee out.'

Her visitor nodded. Marcie dawdled along to the kitchen, not wishing to hurry anything. Hoping, in fact, that when she closed the kitchen door behind her Beth would disappear and never be seen again. She filled the kettle, spooned out the coffee and, while waiting for the water, set a little tray with milk, sugar, and half a dozen of the little breakfast muffins she had baked the day before. And don't forget the butter, she told herself. By which time the water was hot. The coffee was quickly made and, with dragging feet, she struggled back out to the atrium with the load.

Beth was not in her chair. In fact, she was over in the far corner of the room, pawing through the dozen unframed paintings resting against the wall. When Marcie appeared the other woman stopped what she was doing and came back to the coffee table. I wish I could sit down like that, Marcie told herself. This woman moves with the grace of a gazelle. Maybe being short *is* a help.

'Lovely house,' commented Beth. 'I didn't think I could like something like this—claustrophobia, you know. I didn't realise there would be so much light— so much spaciousness. May I see over the whole house?'

'And why not?' Marcie sighed. They took their coffee mugs with them, and the other girl also took her second muffin along. The tour lasted a full half-hour until they came, full circle, back to the coffee table. Beth sank down gracefully into her chair without spilling a drop from her half-filled coffee mug. Marcie approached the divan much more cautiously, and with good reason. Her toe caught under the edge of the rug, and brown coffee spread lavishly. The other woman tittered. Marcie glared, but she mopped up the mess and refilled their mugs.

'A very lovely house.' How can she still talk while she's on her third muffin? Marcie asked herself. If that were me, nothing sensible would come out of my mouth. Why does this petite little thing make me feel so darn awkward?

'You do have title to the house, of course?' asked Beth coldly.

'I—title?'

'Do you legally own the house?'

'Oh. Well, yes and no—I can't really say,' said Marcie. 'Mr Vanderpol did say that I was the only claimant. Uncle Jack died without making a will, you see. So he—he's the lawyer handling the estate—said I could make use of the place for as long as I wanted, because when they go into some court—I forget which——'

'Probate,' the blonde offered. Definitely bored with my lack of legal skill, Marcie thought, but she's hanging in there. It almost seems as if she wants to find out something. What?

'He did say that it would take a long time to settle things,' she sighed, 'and that I shouldn't expect anything drastic to happen.'

'And so you're camping out here with your brush and easel?'

'I guess you could say that.'

'Too bad,' shrugged Beth.

'Too bad?'

'Yes. If you had title to the house, John and I would love to make you an offer for it. It's just the thing we need for a honeymoon hideaway. Close enough to the city, far enough away to avoid the crowds.'

She could have talked on for hours without a word coming through. Marcie had shut down all her senses right after that word 'honeymoon'. The woman might just as well have clubbed her on the back of her head. Honeymoon. 'You and John?' she queried.

'Yes, we've been planning it for some time. Our families are next-door neighbours. You know, there's a lot of truth in the old cliché that men marry the girl next door.'

'Do they really?' Not much of a remark, but the best Marcie could do in the circumstances. The woman opposite felt no need for words. She settled back in her chair, cuddling the coffee mug in her two hands. A large part of a trial lawyer's skill lay in reading faces, and she knew she had scored a major *coup*. In fact, perhaps a *coup de grâce*!

To watch the pair of them, one might think they were friends, sharing coffee in companionable silence. But under those long strands of brown hair, Marcie's mind was busy trying to design a safe way to murder her guest. Boiling in oil was being discarded when Beth put her mug down and stood up.

'I really must be on my way,' she said. 'I *do* think you ought to reconsider the cooking detail. I'm sure I could arrange for John to pay you for your work. Never muzzle the oxen, and all that?'

'I don't think so,' Marcie returned stubbornly. 'I don't feel very ox-ish these days.'

'Well, in that case, I suspect we won't meet again very soon. It's been a pleasure.'

I'll bet it has! Marcie mumbled to herself as she followed the smaller woman out to the door. I wonder if Lucretia Borgia was a blonde, she thought, as she watched the little car drive down the hill.

What with the active morning, and the delightful visit, Marcie was in all kinds of bad humour as noon came and went. She managed to burn her own lunch, found that her garbage pail was full to overflowing, knocked over her easel, and burned her finger on the kettle. Of all the difficulties, the garbage pail was the worse. At her home in Queens, men came by with a big truck twice a week and picked up garbage, but she was willing to bet they didn't come as far north as the Adirondacks. So what *do* you do with garbage? She asked in the wrong place; the spring had no answer. She huddled beside it forlornly, her bag of garbage in her hands. When in doubt, go and ask, she told herself firmly. She dashed back to the house, changed into the most demure dress she owned, tied the neck of the garbage bag with her only spare shoelace, and climbed into the jeep. It had been under-utilised lately, and complained bitterly when she tried the ignition, but she was angry enough with the world not to put up with mechanical nonsense. She got out, kicked all four tyres, and tried again. It worked, as she knew it must.

It was difficult bouncing down that road. Bad enough when you had two hands to drive with, but doing it with one while using the other to keep the garbage bag from falling over was asking a great deal. So she was going slowly when she came around the bend to the fence, and the gate, which was a lucky thing. The gate was closed. She slammed on the brakes, but even at her slow speed the rear of the vehicle skidded around. She turned off the ignition and climbed out, shaking her head angrily. What idiot would close the gate? Only John's grandfather, and *he* couldn't possibly have driven all the way up here just to do that dirty trick.

She stomped stiff-legged over to the gate and reached for its top handle. Nothing moved when she tugged. A giant padlock swung gently back and forth, hooking the ends of the large-mesh metal chain that held the gate shut. The sound of a motor heralded somebody else coming up the mountain. Marcie Waters stood in the middle of the road, shaking the gate in vain, so angry that the top of her head blew off.

'Hey, what's going on, Marcie?' asked John Harley, climbing out of his old truck and walking over to the gate, not realising that Mount Vesuvius was about to erupt all over this little corner of the Adirondacks.

'Marcie?' A puzzled tone. 'I need to talk to you about——'

'Talk?' she gibbered. 'Talk? Why, you rotten——' Her mouth just could not keep up with all the traffic she was trying to force through it; out of the tremendous jam-up she barely managed to splutter.

'How in the world did the gate get locked?' Still walking on the edge of a precipice, he came over to the gate. She had stopped shaking it, and was now standing still with both hands on the padlock, shivering so much that the chain jingled. 'And I don't have a key on me,' he said.

Key! That did it. 'I'll key you,' she managed, and walked angrily back to her jeep.

'Marcie, hey, wait! I——'

There was no care for the rubbish sack. The jeep roared back up the hill in second gear, spewing gravel and dust in all directions. The usual ten-minute trip took four, and when the jeep screeched to a halt beside the bulldozer all four tyres seemed to be smoking. Marcie was talking to herself as she transferred into the cab of the little bulldozer. The diesel engine caught on the first turn. She pulled on the levers to raise the blade in front, then carefully manipulated clutch and movement controls until the little monster was rolling.

Steadily, bouncing, twisting, she hung on to the

controls. By the time she was halfway to her goal she had run out of both English and Arabic words. She screeched them to the high heavens—even the blue jays dared not hurl back a defiance—and some of the words, she blushed to admit, were not even fit for the camel trade. When she came around the final bend, John was standing at the fence, trying to jimmy the lock.

He looked up as the little bulldozer confronted him. 'Oh, my God, Marcie,' he exclaimed. 'Not that! I'll get it——'

Whatever he meant to get, he hardly had a chance to say. He could see Marcie's face through the patches of dirt on the windscreen, and he needed no other message about her intent. He jumped madly for the side of the road, and was barely missed when she dropped the dozer blade and drove full tilt for the nearest fence-post.

When the moving blade struck the deep-set post the bulldozer almost came to a stop, but Marcie juggled the clutch and the accelerator. The machine moved again, pushing hard, until, with a grinding groan, the cedar post pulled loose from its hole. The diesel engine growled with glee, and plunged on down the road, dragging pole, gate, and several feet of wire with it. Marcie disengaged the engine for thinking time. There wasn't much—time, that was. One hurried glance over her shoulder reported that John was dashing down the hill in her direction and from the look on his face, his mission was not reconciliation.

There *had* to be some lever to make the thing back up, but she hadn't the time to look for it. She let out he clutch again, and swung the machine in a wide circle, bouncing off the road into the pine trees, and out again, facing uphill. John took one more look, and for the second time dived for the safety of the bushes. She roared by him triumphantly, ignoring his bellow to stop.

It seemed to be easier going up than coming down. Familiarity, Marcie told herself. I am now a skilled and proficient bulldozer operator. I wonder if that's what they call it? She caressed the levers now, rather than clinging to them. Her foot on the accelerator pedal was commanding. She even remembered to raise the dozer blade when she came back to the road, and she won the race back up to the top of the hill, swinging the machine up next to her jeep.

But John wasn't too far behind. His truck roared in beside her as she stood at the jeep's door, and he vaulted from the cab. 'You crazy damn woman!' he shouted at her. 'You could have *killed* me—and yourself!'

'Too bad!' she yelled back at him. 'Get off my land! I've had you darn Harleys up to my eyeballs today. Go on, get off my land!'

'You aren't fit to be allowed out of the nursery,' he returned. 'I'll get off your land when I damn well please. Now tell me what's going on here!'

'You know what's going on here,' she snapped. 'First you send your little blonde "cousin" up here to read me the Riot Act, and then you padlock the gate so I can't get down the hill. What did you think I would do? Stay up here, out of your way, and fade away into a ghost!'

'Now that's enough!' he grated, stepping closer. 'Get hold of yourself, Marcie. You're hysterical, woman!' Both his hands fell on her shoulders and he gave her a gentle shake to emphasise his statement. It didn't help.

Shaken beyond control, she leaned back and screamed at him. From the bottom of her lungs it came, deep-seated, loaded with anguish that words could not express, compounded with the just-realised dangers of what she had done. Over and over it poured, until her voice could sustain it no longer, and the screams babbled away into hysterical choking coughs.

It all caught him off balance. He stood there, his hands still on her shoulders, a startled expression on his bronze face. 'Marcie,' he said, over and over, without effect. And then one of his huge hands came up and slapped her on the side of her face.

It was like being hit in the face with a bucket of iced water. The physical shock was nothing; the mental was all. In all her young life Marcie Waters had been struck only twice; both times had been at the hands of the hijackers. Once when she had first defied them, and again when, minutes from freedom, she had catalogued all their crimes in lyric Arabic in front of the local television cameras. And now his hand, bringing it all back.

She collapsed against the body of the jeep, squirming to get away from him, her eyes like those of a fawn trapped by the mountain lion. John pulled away from her, dropped his hands and moved back a half pace. 'Dammit, Marcie,' he sighed. 'I didn't mean to—I——'

She licked her lips, still in the grip of terror, still partially located far away, under Beirut's shadow mountains. Her hand moved to her cheek where the blow had landed, and she rubbed it slightly.

'Don't look at me like that,' he pleaded. 'I thought—— You were hysterical, Marcie. I *had* to do it.'

'Yes,' she managed through tight lips. 'That's what they all say. All those men who—who think because they're stronger they have the right to do anything they want. Yes. "I had to do it." That's what they all say.'

'Marcie! I don't know where you're coming from, Marcie. It was something I—I'm sorry. What more can I say?'

'Nothing,' she groaned. 'You've said enough.'

'Marcie,' he pleaded again, 'I don't know what's been going on with you today but believe me, I didn't padlock the gate, and I didn't send Beth up here at any time. When she came back and told me that you were giving up our cooking arrangement, I thought—well, I thought something must have happened, so I came as soon as I could get my grandfather settled. Believe me, Marcie!'

'Oh, is that what you want! You lock me in, you hit me, and now you want to spread a few words of repentance around?' She had managed to control her shivering, to bring herself fully back to this one place. Her temper was under control, but barely. And had Saint Peter come up the mountain to swear to this man's character, she wouldn't have believed him either.

'Would you like to do something for me? she asked bitterly.

'Hell, Marcie,' he returned, 'I'd do most anything for you.'

'How noble!' she grated. 'How about this? Get off my mountain. And take this with you!' She reached into the jeep for the bag of garbage and thrust it at him, then stalked by him into the house. And just to be sure she locked the door behind her.

CHAPTER SIX

THE rains came that night. Soft rains, floating like mist, stirred gently by the southerly breezes. The temperature plummeted from a daytime eighty in the sun, to just over sixty degrees. Marcie shivered in her lightweight nightgown, and was considerably relieved when she climbed out of bed in the morning to feel that the little hot-water radiators scattered through all the rooms were warming up. She managed a quick shower, then dressed in heavy slacks, a wool sweater she had knitted herself, and a shawl.

A dismal morning can be lightened by a good breakfast, and Marcie threw herself into the preparation. Scrambled eggs, a slice or two of honey-cured ham, toast, and coffee. As she searched for ingredients she looked in the freezer and began to feel guilty. John had paid for all that food, and she had cut him off by refusing to cook for him any further. That was resolution number one: to return to him everything he had paid for. But first, she had to go down and buy herself something to keep *her* going. Repayment certainly doesn't mean I have to starve myself, she lectured herself. Which was enough of a palliative to her conscience to allow her to sit down and enjoy her breakfast.

Despite her resolve her feet were dragging. She poked and pottered around the kitchen, cleaning up, used the carpet sweeper in every room in the house, and picked up the things in her bedroom. Some of the rooms she felt as though she was seeing for the first time. The house was actually bigger than she had originally thought, with five separate bedrooms, as well as a room that must have served Uncle Jack as his library. It was shelved from floor to ceiling, and well-stocked. By eleven o'clock, however, she could find no further reason to procrastinate.

There was still a light drizzle falling, and the roof of her jeep was not exactly waterproof. She snatched up her little plastic poncho, checked her bag for money and chequebook, and dashed out of the door. Her windscreen wiper was not functioning too well, and the dusty road down the hill had become muddy and slippery. When she reached the bottom she stopped for a moment to catch her breath.

The old logging road was easier to drive on— unpaved, but packed down hard from years of handling heavy trucks. Her heart gave a little jump as she passed the entry road to the lakeside, but she resolutely applied her foot to the accelerator pedal and went on, along Route Three, past the long line of motels and the shopping centre, over the railroad tracks again. She just did not want to stop in Tupper Lake to shop; it held too many memories. She circled back up the hill and headed for Saranac Lake.

But it was the little community around Flower Lake that attracted her. Back in the narrow streets behind the waterfront was an A&P. Probably it was because there was one nearby her home in Queens, she told herself, but for whatever reason she went in, shopped frugally for herself, and cringed at the dent it put in her purse. 'Now I can go and face him,' she told herself grimly. But she was not even surprised when the jeep, without her direction, turned towards Lake Placid rather than back towards Spring Mountain.

She idled through that larger community, pleased at the clean quiet appearance, astonished that Olympic advertisements still plastered the area; she gawked at

FIRST-CLASS ROMANCE

Mail This Heart TODAY!

And We'll Deliver:

**4 FREE BOOKS
A FREE MANICURE SET
PLUS
A SURPRISE MYSTERY BONUS
TO YOUR DOOR!**

See Inside For More Details →

HARLEQUIN DELIVERS FIRST-CLASS ROMANCE— DIRECT TO YOUR DOOR

Mail the Heart sticker on the postpaid order card today and you'll receive:

—4 new Harlequin Romance novels—FREE
—a beautiful manicure set—FREE
—and a surprise mystery bonus—FREE

But that's not all. You'll also get:

Money-Saving Home Delivery
When you subscribe to Harlequin Romance, the excitement, romance and faraway adventures of these novels can be yours for previewing in the convenience of your own home at less than retail prices. Every month we'll deliver 8 new books right to your door. If you decide to keep them, they'll be yours for only $1.99 each. That's 26¢ less per book than what you pay in stores. And there is no extra charge for shipping and handling!

Free Monthly Newsletter
It's the indispensable insider's look at our most popular writers and their upcoming novels. Now you can have a behind-the-scenes look at the fascinating world of Harlequin! It's an added bonus you'll look forward to every month!

Special Extras—FREE
Because our home subscribers are our most valued readers, we'll be sending you additional free gifts from time to time as a token of our appreciation.

OPEN YOUR MAILBOX TO A WORLD OF LOVE AND ROMANCE EACH MONTH. JUST COMPLETE, DETACH AND MAIL YOUR FREE OFFER CARD TODAY!

You'll love your beautiful manicure set—
an elegant and useful accessory, compact
enough to carry in your handbag. Its rich
burgundy case is a perfect expression of
your style and good taste—and it's yours
free with this offer!

Remember! To receive your free books, manicure set and mystery gift, return the postpaid card below. But don't delay!

DETACH AND MAIL CARD TODAY.

If offer card has been removed, write to: Harlequin Reader Service, 901 Fuhrmann Blvd., P.O. Box 1394, Buffalo, NY 14240-1394 the delightful architecture of the local high school, and stopped dead in front of Sears & Roebuck. How about that for nostalgia? she sighed. Home, sweet home is represented by a Sears store! She smothered a wry laugh, parked, and went in to browse.

That was all she meant to do, but browsing carries its own penalty. They were displaying inflatable rubber boats. One especially caught her eye, a tiny two-seater shaped something like a canoe, with a foot-pump to inflate it. It was a cute little thing, 'and I have ripper—whatever he said—rights on the lake,' Marcie told herself and the amused saleswoman. 'I can go on that darn lake any time I want to, and right in front of him, too!' To which the saleswoman agreed as she bundled up the package. Her elderly smile might have been much wider had she known the thought that ran through Marcie's mind as an addition. 'And there's a heck of a lot better feeling to doing it that way. I can drive over and put my boat in my water and enjoy myself, instead of sneaking up like a bandit just to return all his food! And the food bit can be just a sort of "oh, by the way" affair.'

Overwhelmed by her own logic, she drove back home, humming a little tune as she went. The rain had stopped completely, which just fitted into her plans. One could hardly expect to go boating in the rain— well, no sensible person could, she thought. And in addition, the path up the mountain was so slippery that another inch of rain would have left her stuck at the bottom.

She pulled the jeep up in front of the door. Unloading her few packages took but a moment; re-loading the contents of the freezer in the vehicle took considerably longer. By two o'clock she was finished. The appearance of the sun made her sweater redundant. She changed into a T-shirt which featured a power boat on its breast, and the words 'Sail me to Savanna' around the design.

Feeling more like an avenging knight, Marcie climbed into the jeep and navigated her way down to the road, and over to *his* entrance trail, where she stopped. 'Get your head straight,' she told herself. 'Why are you doing all this?' Because—because. I just don't know, do I? she argued. He hurt me. And that's almost impossible, unless he means more to me than just a casual neighbour. Or perhaps I'm suffering from a little infatuation? He never asked anything of me, or promised me anything. Just that big smile, and those darn kisses. Nothing more. Which left a bigger hole in my heart than I had before. You're a fool, Marcie Waters. He's only a man; there must be a hundred million of them in the United States. With a choice like that, why are you so darn concerned about *one*? Just this one?

You're acting like a silly little duckling. No sooner do you burst out of your egg than you're—what do they call it?—imprinted by the first moving male in sight? Lord, what a simple stupidity that would be—if true. I could more easily believe that I've fallen in love with—oh, God!

Sobered, perhaps even a little more depressed, she thumped on the steering wheel. And I haven't any idea what *he* thinks, she continued. But Elizabeth Fortin, she's got the explanation, and deep down inside you really believe what she said, Marcie. Now what?

Now I'll—now—all that meat's unfreezing on the back seat, and that's as good an excuse as any. Go on with the original plan. At least that way you'll get to see him one more time. That would be nice.

Quickly, before logic made her change her mind, she started the motor again and bounced along the road that wound round the base of the mountain, skirted the sandy beach of Spring Lake, and parked in the shade of the pine trees a dozen feet or so from the entrance to the log cabin.

There was a quiet in this mountain cove unlike that at the top of the hill. Up there the breeze blew freely, down here it wandered through pines, rattling the needles, picking up their scent. Up there the world beckoned from mountain-top to mountain-top. Down here the view was of the lake: placid, hardly wind-rippled. Smoke drifted in tiny tendrils from the two chimneys that pierced the roof of the building. it was hard to call it just a log cabin. The building was a sizeable ranch-style house that happened to be built of logs. She climbed out of the jeep, smoothed down her T-shirt, and clumped up the stairs to the open veranda

'And what do *you* want?' Elizabeth Fortin. Marcie gritted her teeth. What she wanted to say was, 'I've come all this way to knock you on your lovely bottom.' But of course that's not the type of thing that nice young ladies say. She was getting very tired of being a nice young lady.

'I want to see John Harley,' she said.

'Do you really? Why?' It wasn't curiosity riding on Beth's tone, it was vitriol.

'That's strictly private business,' Marcie returned, struggling not to rise to the bait. Her last encounter with this Harley 'cousin' was still hot in her mind. The other woman stared her up and down as if she were a day-old fish at the market.

'Johnny!' She opened the screen door and was calling into the depths of the house. Footsteps stirred. John appeared at the door, brushing by Beth, unsmiling.

'Yes?'

'I——' stuttered Marcie. 'I brought you the food you paid for.'

'In the jeep?'

She nodded. He came down the steps and started towards the vehicle. She followed. Beth stayed on the porch, by the door. By the vehicle, out of earshot of the house, he turned around and waited for Marcie to catch up. 'I wish you wouldn't do this,' he said softly.

'I——' She could find nothing to say. He looked ten years older, with fatigue lines across his forehead, and a worried look in his deep blue eyes. Even the bronze tone of his skin and hair seemed muted. She was silenced by the tug at her heart.

'I miss you,' he went on. 'Yesterday was painful. Today is worse.

'I don't see why,' she returned. 'Unless your girlfriend can't cook?'

'She's *not* my girlfriend,' he said, and then a little smile ticked at the corner of his mouth. 'And no, she can't cook. I thought I'd die after last night! Burned pork chops.' And then, with a little dramatic mockery in his voice, 'If you care anything about me, Marcie, you'll rescue me from this slow death.' It was the wrong kind of joke, as far as Marcie was concerned.

'I brought you all the food in the freezer,' she said coldly. 'You'll have to send someone to pick up your equipment.' And don't you think, John Harley, that just because I love you so much I'll fall for *that* old line. I don't intend playing odd woman out in your sex life. She meant it all, but hadn't the courage to tell him so, face to face.

He shrugged. 'That's the way you feel about it?'

'That's the way.'

He reached into the back seat and picked up a load of frozen meat. Her hands reached in at the same time to pull out her packaged boat. They touched. John dropped the meat. Sparks shot up her arm—emotional shocks, of such intensity that she was shaken and drew back. He remained in place, staring at the hand she had touched, showing nothing on his face. The tableau held for a minute, and then for two.

'What's the matter?' Beth called down from the porch. Her voice had lost its smoothness; the shrill tone was jealousy. It snapped the two of them out of their daze. Marcie walked around to the other side of the jeep to establish her personal boundaries. John grinned at her, and set about emptying the vehicle.

The boat package contained a list of instructions, geared for any ten-year-old mind, but Marcie struggled with it for half an hour, and was almost in tears when she finally hit the right combination. The foot pump helped. The steady up-and-down work not only filled out the rubber boat to its right size, but the labour involved proved cathartic. She slumped down on the sand when the last instruction was completed. it looked like a boat. It felt like a boat. *Ergo*, it *was* a boat. Basic logic that even a lawyer might recognise. She walked back to the jeep to pick up her packed lunch and her water bottle.

John was waiting at the vehicle. 'What the devil are you up to now?' he asked.

'I'm going for a ride in my boat,' she snapped. 'I would think that was obvious.'

'That's a boat?'

'Of course that's a boat. Only lawyers and bank robbers can afford a wooden boat these days!'

'You say that as if you thought they both fit in one category.' That soft grin, reflected in those deep eyes. Marcie felt a little chill, a haunted feeling, as if something was walking over her grave.

'I don't want to argue with you, Mr Harley,' she sighed. 'I know it may be distasteful for you to share the lake with your former cook, but you did say I had rights to the water. Do you own some particular drops or do we share them all in kind?'

'My,' he said solemnly. 'First it was chilly on top of the mountain, and now it's turned the same down here. Look here, Marcie Waters.' He took the one step needed to close the distance between them, and held both her elbows. 'Just because you're a snob, lady, you don't have to infer the same thing of me. You are *not* my former cook. And even if you were I would be pleased to share the lake with you. Or anything else, for that matter. Just what do you want from me?'

'I want you to let me go!' she snapped. 'Your girlfriend is watching from the porch. She might get the wrong idea.'

'On the other hand,' returned John, 'she might get the *right* idea for a change.' She struggled futilely as he pulled her close, hard up against his chest. Struggling became more difficult than before, because now she was where she wanted to be, no matter what her mind told her. Her hands beat at his shoulders for a moment, then paused; her fists opened and rested on either side of his face. When the kiss came gently to her it savoured of all the joys of earth. She relaxed her guard and slid down into the deep wells of love and satisfaction.

It was not contentment she fell into, but rather excitement. The flares of feeling that just his lips initiated were followed by strings of firecrackers as his hands moved in wide circles on her back. Warmth, passion, love—fear? The last flashed into her mind as John gradually released her. Fear. Fear that he didn't mean all his body promised. Fear that he *did* mean it, but it was only lust. Fear.

Her hands beat against him again, about as effectively as if they were butterfly wings, but he released her anyway, and stepped back. He wore a big grin this time, as if he knew he had won, but could bide his time. She felt an instant hatred for him—for all men. What gives him the right to hold me by passion? she screamed at herself, and, feeling the pain, she turned and ran down the beach.

Luckily her boat was lightweight. She slid it into the water and scrambled in after it, doing her best to keep her weight in the centre, as the instruction book prescribed. As if the devil were behind her she paddled. Inexpertly, of course; there aren't many places in Queens for a middle-income girl to learn paddling. The boat moved awkwardly, but move it did, and Marcie was almost two hundred feet from the shore when she finally made sense of what he was saying. He was jumping up and down beside the rickety pier, waving something over his head.

She stopped and rested on her paddle, debating. 'Your lunch,' he was shouting. 'You forgot your lunch!'

And maybe I'll just go without, she thought. Maybe I can spend a whole day on the water without eating. They both of them keep telling me I'm overweight. I could do without the calories, and it's safe to keep my distance from that man! But he has my water bottle too. I don't think I could go the day very comfortably without. I'd better go back.

And so she did, paddling slowly. The stroke dropped even lower than before when she saw Beth come down the veranda stairs and join him on the beach. One light stroke at a time, watching as the bow of her tiny craft bounded from side to side off her line of approach. One stroke at a time as her fertile mind dragged up sixty ways to murder one or both of them, and sixty-five ways to commit suicide in such a way that they would be blamed. Daydreams. She recognised them as such, and pushed them out of the way. It did nothing for her emotional index, but her vision cleared, and the little boat slid up on the sand about four feet away from both of them.,

'You seem to have forgotten your water,' said John in a casually conversational tone of voice. But he made not a move to come closer.

'And your sandwiches,' Beth chimed in. 'We wouldn't want you to be hungry out there on the lake while we're having *coq au vin*.'

'You could bring it to me?' Marcie asked quietly. John shook his head, but held out the bottle. Marcie shook her head in disgust and struggled out of the boat. It was harder getting out than getting in.

'I don't feel *that* proud!' laughed Beth. She walked over to the boat and put the sandwiches down on the rear thwart. Marcie's eyes were glued to the water bottle—or to him, perhaps. She was still so confused that she wasn't really sure. She walked slowly over to him and put out a hand.

'You're sure you want this?'

'Of course I'm sure,' she snapped. 'Why must you always be a—teaser?'

'That wasn't the word you meant to use,' he chuckled.

'No,' she admitted, 'but nice girls don't say that sort of word. Give me the darn bottle.'

'Not for nothing.' He held the bottle up above his head, a long way out of her reach. Marcie started a quick kick in the direction of his kneecap, but remembered in time that she was barefoot.

'Damn you,' she muttered under her breath. Her clenched fists hung at her sides; her pale face was red with anger. And John was laughing.

'What was that you said? I thought nice girls didn't say things like that.'

'Well, you forced me to,' she raged. 'Give—me—my—bottle!'

'Oh, for heaven's sake, John, give the girl her bottle,' Beth said crossly. She was still over by the boat, behind their backs.

'Of course,' he said solemnly. 'Just as soon as I get paid my finder's fee.'

'What in—what is that?' Marcie was almost in tears. He saw and relented—almost.

'That's the fee any good lawyer gets for finding things,' he said. 'One kiss.'

'For heaven's sake!' snapped Beth.

'I——' Marcie studied his face. He meant it. And there wasn't a sign of malice in his face. It almost looked as if it meant something to him, this blackmail kiss. Her heart wanted to respond; her mind cautioned. She compromised, stretching up on her toes, pulling his head down as far as she could, and kissing him on the cheek. And then a quick release and two steps backward.

'Hey,' he laughed, 'that's not quite what I had in mind, but I guess it meets the contract terms!' He handed her the water bottle, and she snatched at it, unwilling to be under his hand again. 'Be careful out there. Lakes can be dangerous for solitary boaters.' Again that solemn caring face, as if he really felt that way.

It was too difficult for her to equate what he said with what she knew. She backed away from him, stumbling into the side of the boat which Beth had already launched. There was nothing solemn or caring in the other girl's face. Nothing at all. If she had been taking reservations for the *Titanic*, Marcie would have been the first passenger she signed up. But Marcie was too startled, too dazed, to know. She flashed a grateful smile at the other woman, stepped over the side into her boat, and settled back as Beth gave the craft a shove out into deeper water.

Paddling seemed easier this time. She discovered the trick of trailing her paddle after every stroke, using it as a rudder. The boat rode slightly lower in the water than before, but not enough to be worrisome. Behind her she heard him call again, but she was determined, and kept her back to the shore.

The house was at the narrow section of the lake, in the middle of the letter 'C' which the lake resembled. After a half-hour of paddling she was out of sight around the curve, out into the broader section of water. She stopped to rest her arms. Painting required arm and muscle control, but not the same muscles as paddling. And sitting in the middle of a rubber boat would seem to be an ideal position, but it wasn't.

A small breeze had sprung up, pushing the boat up-lake at a slow but steady pace. It seemed such a good idea, to lean back and let Mother Nature do the paddling. Ahead of her was a tiny tree-covered island, and the shores on either side were receding from her. Farther off, towering above the lake, was the bald peak of Rice Mountain. A flock of birds were circling up there, too far away to be recognised. A high bone-chilling howl echoed from the hills on either side of her, so confusing that she could not exactly locate its source. An eastern coyote, a product of experimenting with nature. A few true coyote had been brought east and turned loose; the Adirondack region, and all the mountains of Vermont and New Hampshire, across the Hudson River, were the targets of their invasion.

The wind was enough to move the boat and to keep the mosquitoes off. The black flies which had tormented her on her first trip had disappeared. He had promised that, hadn't he? She could hardly suppress the smile. He was right in so many ways, with so many things; why couldn't he be right about love?

She leaned back, stretching out completely after a moment, with her head on the rubber coaming of the craft, and her feet up in the narrow prow. Sky and clouds and a bird or two. All peaceful and quiet. Her mind drifted. What if——

What if we married, John and I? The little church— I don't exactly know where—my long white dress, with Miriam crying and Hafez cheering from the side. I walk down the aisle, and John is waiting, and the minister comes in. John is saying 'I do', but his grandfather shouts, 'No, he doesn't,' and grabs him and pulls him away. I run after them both, screaming, and Beth trips me and throws a bucket of water in my face, and —— Water in my face?

Her eyes snapped open. There was water in her face, splashing over the side of the little boat, the side that was hardly a half-inch above the level of the lake. The boat was shrinking—the boat was sinking! Marcie sat up cautiously and looked around. The little island was about two hundred feet in front of her. The nearer shore looked to be a quarter of a mile away, and a little stream of bubbles was pulsing up through the water from the back of the boat. Bubbles. Air. Escaping air.

The tension was building up fast. Her throat was blocked by it, and her mind spun. For a fruitless moment she searched over the side with one hand, trying to stop the flow of bubbles. Wherever the leak was, it eluded her. So move the boat, her mind commanded. If you can't stop the leak, get to the island. It's been a long time since you passed the YWCA swimming test, and that was only a hundred feet!

As the adrenalin surged she snatched up the paddle and bent her back to it. The little waterlogged craft responded heavily, barely improving over the headway that the wind had provided. She was committed to the course; there seemed to be no other way to go. She tucked in her chin and kept at it, applying all the muscle that her long frame had to give. Stroke after stroke, as the water level crept higher along the side. Stroke after stroke, until finally the water seeped into the boat. First a drop or two, then a dribble, and at last a flood. The well of the boat filled, and still she sat. The rubber boat was beneath the water, but still retained some buoyancy. Enough at least to give her a chance to think—a chance to prepare.

There wasn't much to be done, swimming was the only alternative. She needed to go without handicap. The T-shirt came off with no trouble, but the heavy jeans required more effort. Which left her with only a pair of lace briefs to her naGe. But her name was not what she was trying to save. Stripped for action, she fumbled for the water bottle, swinging it over her head and down her back. It was time to go.

No jumping was required; all she had to do was lie down on her stomach and push off. The bright yellow of the rubber boat fell behind her, restored to some height when her weight was taken off. Lord knows how long it might float without her, she thought. And that was all the time she had for thought.

Her one swimming asset was an awkward sidestroke. She started off doggedly, stopping every few strokes to look up and ahead, to be sure she was on course. Her strength was as great as any woman's her age, but her proficiency was terrible. More than once she managed to gulp a mouthful of water, and had to roll over on her back to clear her choked throat. But the island was closer—measurably closer. And each time she caught her breath she rolled over on her side again and gave it all the strength, all the courage, that she could muster.

Her past drove her on. It had been like that on the aeroplane. Worn to exhaustion when the two assassins had shot the one boy and turned towards the other, she had found a well of strength, jumped between them and their victim, and dared them to shoot her first. They had been astonished. First, because she spoke a lyrically perfect Arabic, and second, because she had challenged them in the Prophet's name to kill a woman. To take up the shame of killing a woman. And while they had struggled with their convictions she had quoted for them verse after verse from the *Siva* of the *Koran* named *Nissa*, 'The Women' and the Commentaries, until finally the tougher of them had muttered 'Ya Bint' in that disgusted tone, and Marcie knew she had won!

And I'm going to win now, she promised herself. Going to win. Going to win. But she needed a rest, and had not the strength to roll over on her back, she took a deep breath, put her head down into the water, and floated. There seemed to be patterns in the lake bottom, she could see. She kicked her legs aimlessly. Patterns. Her nose came up to one of them and she was aground. She lay there for another endless moment, dazed, half-dreaming, before her mind kicked her into raising her head.

The first breath she took was torture. The air screamed down her windpipe as if it were fire. There was some water trapped somewhere. She coughed it up and felt better. The air cooled. She was safe.

Her luck had guided her to a shallow sandy beach on the west side of the island. The closest point that she could have hoped to achieve, and she knew that achieving it had nothing to do with her skill. Something—someone—had guided her. She staggered up out of the water and collapsed on the white sand, giving thanks in two languages to He who watched. Exhausted, she rolled up in a little foetal ball and promptly fell asleep.

It was hard to tell what woke her up. The sun was close to the mountain tops to the west, the breeze had fallen away, and it was getting chilly. Marcie forced herself to stand up. Her legs were weak, shaking. She moved closer to one of the pine trees, and steadied herself against it, on higher ground. She brushed futilely at the sand that covered her. 'When you dry off it will fall off,' she told herself firmly, but it was hard to ignore. It itched and rubbed. When her legs appeared strong enough she took a few steps around the curve of the beach. There were a few splashes as fish jumped just offshore, but nothing else broke the mirror-smooth surface of the lake. She took a sip from the water bottle, then laughed at herself. Not only for conserving the water so carefully, but for having gone back into *his* trap at the very beginning.

'Where do you suppose they get their water from, Marcie?' she asked herself in a strained little-girl voice. 'From the lake, you idiot! Where do you get *your* water? From the spring. And where does the lake get its water? From the spring! When a more stupid woman is born in the world, I'll bet her name will be Marcie Waters!' With which she pulled the cork on the water bottle and poured it over her head.

It wasn't quite enough to get all the sand off. She giggled as she made her way down into the chilly water and thoroughly rinsed herself off. The giggle was on the ragged edge of hysteria, and she knew it. Clean but cold, she staggered back up out of the lake, and found herself a fallen log behind the beach. She was sitting there when she heard the call again.

Again! That was what had woken her up. Somebody shouting. She was too tired to get up, but she did manage a fairly adequate scream. Then the voice again. 'Marcie! Damn it, woman, make another noise so I can tell which way!'

Strange, when one is tired beyond recall, how hard it is to make a simple decision. Make another noise? She swallowed a couple of times, her throat dry. Make another noise. Dutifully she called, 'Over here'. It came out as some sort of rusty croak.

'Marcie!' John Harley. That deep, wonderful, welcoming voice. My John. 'Make a noise, Marcie!' he yelled at the top of his voice. My John. And there was only one way to make it. She leaned back, filled her lungs, and screamed loudly enough to make the mountain lion, on the lake shore across the way, lope off into the brush.

'OK, love, I'm coming!' Like a bull roaring. OK, love? She toyed with the phrase, too worn to understand it, but not so worn that she could not inspect it—repeat it—let it ring in her ears as if he meant it.

'Lord, I'd love to be loved,' she sighed, and then slipped off the log in a faint.

She had no idea how long it had lasted. It was the second faint of her life. The first had occurred when she was fourteen, when she had cut her finger with a carving knife, and had been overwhelmed by the sight of her own blood. 'So you'll never make a nurse!' Miriam had cried, with one more of her ambitions for her daughter flying out the window. And now there were arms around her, warm and comforting, and something to lay her head against, and it all seemed unreal. 'I never did want to be a nurse, Miriam,' she said softly.

'No, I guess not.' Miriam's voice had acquired a

masculine timbre to it. Marcie forced her eyes open.
'John?'

'I believe so,' he muttered. He was doing something
with his free hand. Drying her off, or something like
that. There were exciting overtones to it, but she was
so tired—so tired.

'What kept you so long?' she muttered, and fell
asleep. He settled back into the sand, cupped her
breast in one hand, and watched over her as the sun
disappeared and the false twilight fell on the land.

CHAPTER SEVEN

JOHN sat with her longer than he had planned, and still debated. His arm was almost asleep from the weight of her. As long as the light lasted he stared. She was not exactly beautiful—not like Beth, or the hundred other women who filled his New York nights. Not beautiful, but wholesome, lovable, compassionate, filled with the sparkle of life. And for all that, far from ugly, either. There was a flame within her that reached out over distance and seared him. He had been shocked at that first meeting. A lawyer holds no brief for the sudden flash of emotions. Kids' stuff, that, nourished by infatuation. But something had happened to him, something that logic could not explain, and it worried him. Now what?

Wake her up and take her back? Or let her have her sleep out and be done with it? Perhaps the latter would be the wiser course. Lord knows, she's suffered enough shocks for one day. Let her lie. His hand ghosted softly over her arm, her stomach, down to her bare thigh, always returning to that place that was his fixation, her warm firm breast. The wind was cool when it resumed after its sunset pause. She shivered unconsciously. She has to be warm, he told himself.

As a temporary measure he slipped off his own safari shirt and wound it around her. She was tall, for a girl, but his shirt went around her twice. He laid her back gently against the log, flexed his arm to restore the flow of blood, then eased her down into the sand. As he moved her away from him she stirred and whimpered a protest, then curled up in a ball and slept

113

on. He watched for a time. Her long hair, dry now, fluttered around her elfin face, and John brushed it back gently, with the guilty feeling that somehow he was violating her privacy.

There was so much he had to reconcile. The poison had been fed into his veins throughout his childhood in tiny driblets, meant to condition. Meant to develop his hatred to match his mother's. It had all appeared so simple, so clear-cut, in those days. Nora Waters was responsible for all the agonies, the separations, the limited alimony. Nora Waters, and all her descendants. If it had not been for Nora, his mother and father would still be married—at least that was what he had learned as a child. But now, face to face with reality, he saw that it just was not so. And did his grandfather believe that, too, or did he have some private grief to haunt him? Choices. There had to be choices made, and this was the night to make them. He could have pondered for hours, but need drove. He strode quickly back around the curve of the beach to where the guide-boat waited.

Bringing the boat to her took some time. Although the gentle curve of sand made easy walking, there was a ledge of rock that extended out some distance in the water, and required careful navigation in the dusk. The craft made a crunching noise as he beached it a few feet from where she slept. She stirred again, and he could swear she mumbled his name. He vaulted over the bow and hurried to her. 'It's all right, Marcie,' he assured softly. 'I'm here.'

'I know,' she said very clearly, muttered something else, and drifted off again. John watched for another moment before going back to the boat. As usual, he had loaded the emergency pack into the craft when he had left the cabin. She had been gone far too long, and he had been worried. Something must have happened—not a very nice something, either.

'Don't for goodness' sake worry about her,' Beth had insisted. 'That kind can always take care of themselves. Finish your supper. I spent a great deal of time with it.'

He had looked up quickly at his grandfather, who had quickly looked away. The meal had been a total disaster. Somehow or another the wine basting for the chicken had caught fire. The old man had been muttering under his breath. John had counted to twenty and had sworn a couple of times to himself. 'No, there's something wrong,' he had repeated. 'I have to go!'

'Well, I don't see why,' Beth had argued, following him out of the house.

'No, I don't suppose you do,' John had retorted as he threw the emergency rescue pack into the guide-boat. 'But *I* do.' Under his breath, that last statement. He had rowed up the lake as fast as his arms could take him. The long slender guide-boat, especially built for these waters and these times, had jumped like a racing shell.

What the hell had Beth meant, 'That kind——' His normally cool cousin was really blowing her mind about Marcie. And why? He had sported several women in the past few months, and Beth had only laughed about them. Of course the past bound them together. Growing up with Beth had turned her into his prime confidante, the one to whom he turned with his concerns. Their childhood friendship had gradually developed into something more. A companionship. They dated regularly. His mother thought that Beth would make a perfect wife for an established lawyer and outsiders smelled romance. John knew better, but was willing to drift with the current; marriage, after all, was just another business contract. But a flaw had developed. He normally confided everything to Beth, except for this—this madness with Marcie. And how could you confide something you don't really understand yourself?

He had put his back to the oars again, alternately scanning the shores of the lake on either side. It had almost been by accident that he had recovered his first clue. His port oar had become entangled with something and, when he had raised it to look, he had seen her T-shirt with that idiotic proclamation printed across it, and suddenly there had been a sick feeling in the pit of his stomach. A girl like Marcie didn't lose her shirt by sheer accident. At that point he had shipped both oars and moved up to the bow, scanning the water in front and on both sides.

A gleam of yellow—something had floated ahead of him, just below the surface. He had used one of the oars to scull forward, eyes glued to the yellow patch as he came up alongside it. Her little rubber boat, floating some six or eight inches below the surface, but still floating. He had leaned over the side and pulled it up. Waterlogged, it had weighed over fifty pounds, until it had broken free, and had once again been a light burden. One of the two air compartments had been completely deflated, and the other was just not strong enough to sustain a passenger. He had pulled the cap and plug, let the air drain out, and thrown the limp packet down in the well of the guide-boat. She had to be around here, and the only hope was the island. He had sat down again, unshipped the oars, and pulled mightily in that direction, stopping every few strokes to call for her.

And now here they were, alone in the twilight, and she slept. He walked up the beach, carrying the emergency pack with him. It contained all the usual rescue needs. He unsnapped the covers and rummaged through until he found the two blankets. One he rolled up to make her a pillow; the other he spread over her, and tucked it gently in.

The night was moonless, but the stars abounded. In the wilderness dark, they gleamed like little searchlights, and their reflection off the pure-white sand was enough for him to see by. He forayed into the pines, gathering rocks to build a fire wall out on the beach; a second invasion furnished enough fallen branches for a fire. He lit it, nursed it to a small perfection, then settled down, cross-legged, on sentry duty.

From time to time during the long night he checked on her, and once got up and moved her closer to the fire. She showed a grateful smile, but her eyes remained closed. He sat down again, filled his pipe from his waterproof pouch, and studied her, across the fire. The breeze nipped at his chest, protected only by a thin undershirt. A wandering mosquito stopped off for a quick lunch. He slapped at it absentmindedly, threw a couple more logs on the fire, and leaned back. The flickering flames played tricks with her face—or perhaps, he mused, I'm seeing it clearly for the first time. There was a haunting beauty about it, a peace in repose, a look of promise and faith. And very suddenly he knew he wanted all that. Not for a moment, but for a lifetime. 'You're a crazy fool, Counsellor,' he whispered, 'to fall in love out of the blue like that. And she doesn't even *like* you!' In the distance, from somewhere around the peak of Blue Mountain, two coyotes laughed him to sleep.

Marcie woke up when a slanting beam of sunlight splattered over her eyes and nose. As usual, she came around a piece at a time, opening one eye, stretching one arm, moving tentatively in the bed—which wasn't a bed. The shock penetrated, both eyes snapped open, and she stared, bewildered.

'Well, fancy meeting you here.' A friendly voice, deep, powerful, and associated with the smell of ham and eggs. A nice combination, she concluded quickly, and managed a wavering smile.

'Breakfast in ten minutes,' he continued. 'The bathroom is to your right, madame.'

'Oh, stop it,' she protested weakly. But she did manage to shake herself, stand up, and stretch. Her back muscles ached abominably, as did those of her left thigh. She looked down, and discovered how very much of Marcie Waters was on display through the gaps in his shirt. With a startled gasp she reached for the blanket, and wrapped it around her. Play it lighthearted, her mind told her. 'You said to the right?'

John made a lordly gesture towards the curve in the beach.

'Running water, cold only,' he proclaimed. 'Better hurry before I burn the breakfast.' It was enough warning. She hurried. As he had mentioned, there was plenty of water. A whole lake full. After completing her toilet Marcie tried a few exercises to get her gears back in running order, and then went back to the fire, somewhat cheered.

'The beds in this place leave a lot to be desired,' she told him, 'and now you *are* burning the ham. Is it too much to ask of a lawyer that he be able to cook?'

'Too much.' He relinquished his place and job with a big grin. The fire flared at just that moment. Marcie reached for the tiny frying pan with both hands, and lost her blanket. The food came off the fire easily enough, but to the detriment of her modesty.

'I'm not looking,' he said. 'I'm being a gentleman to the end. Your T-shirt is almost dry. Want it?'

Love is trust, she told herself fiercely, and turned around to face him. He was about four feet away, eyes wide open. So much for trust! She snatched at the garment. Wearing it would cover all the gaps his shirt left. And it's my own, she thought. Why the devil am I making excuses? She turned her back, changed into her T-shirt, put his shirt back on top of it, and went on with the cooking. After all, she told herself primly, I'm covered almost to my knees. What more could I want?

They shared the full meal. She had lost her initial shyness; John's presence was like a balm. She wanted him to know that, and yet she hadn't quite the nerve to watch him while she said so. Looking off across the lake was an acceptable substitute. She pulled up her knees in front of her and clasped them with her arms. 'I—I want to thank you for saving my life.'

'Me? You could have swum to the shore easily enough.'

'I don't think so. I barely made it here to the island.'

'Your life-jacket could have sustained you for another twenty-four hours. I don't see it——'

'I don't have one,' she explained.

'You don't have one! You mean to tell me——'

'No, I didn't mean to tell you at all. I—I didn't think, when I bought the boat. It was all so—sort of——'

'Off the cuff? Spur of the moment.'

'Yes—like that.'

John moved around the circle of the fire and sat down beside her. One arm wrapped itself around her shoulder and she nestled back the tiniest bit to lean against him. 'Not too smart?' he prodded.

'Not about boats. I suppose you've sailed a lot?'

'Most of my life. You?'

'I—— No. I went on the cruise around Manhattan once. And took an airplane to—on a long trip.' And isn't that a devil of a thing to report? she told herself. I've managed to spend my whole life commuting between Queens and Manhattan. Great adventurer! And if Miriam hadn't wanted so badly to go to Lebanon to see her sister Saida I would never have made that trip, never been hijacked, never been thrust out of my little cocoon into the wide world. Poor Aunt Saida, she could just never see me as a real Habib.

'So,' he mused, 'this litle boating exercise was not the smartest thing in the world. Why? Just to teach me a lesson?'

'I—— Yes. You and that—that cousin of yours.'

'Ah. She aggravates you?'

'Both of you do,' she snapped. 'And your grand-father isn't too far behind!' She could feel his shoulder shake, but had no intention of showing that she knew. Laughing, was he? Well, he is in the position to do so—my turn will come later. Now if he as much as mentions 'I told you so' I'll kill him. I swear I will!

John managed to escape death by very wisely saying nothing, although his hand did tighten on her shoulder and pull her back farther against him. It was too pleasant. One can hardly build up wrath and hatred when the enemy is so damnably comforting. She sighed, one of those sighs that start somewhere around the toes and work their way up.

'Feeling a little better?' he asked.

'Yes. Somewhat.'

'We'd better start moving. Somebody at the house will be worrying about us by this time.'

'Like who?' Marcie scowled at the water, unwilling to allow anything from the outside to intrude on this one perfect moment.

'Like my grandfather, that's who.'

'I can't believe it. About your grandfather, I mean. Why does he hate me?'

'I don't know. Maybe he doesn't. All I can tell you is that it's all part of a terrible mess involving your mother and my father. It's been poisoning our family for years, and somehow I mean to put an end to it. Ready to go?'

She held her position for a few quiet minutes, rocking back and forth in the little hollow in which she sat. How stern he is! No way am I ready to go, she told herself. No way. I just want to sit here until doomsday—or until New York City gets a Republican mayor, whichever miracle comes first.

'We have to go.' John stood up, leaving her with no strength to lean against. It was a lonely feeling. 'Marcie?'

'I'm coming.' He pulled her up with one strong hand. She balanced precariously, both legs rebelling. One or two stumbling steps. His hand caught her under her elbow, providing equilibrium. 'It's nothing,' she smiled at him. 'Everything seems to be stiff.'

'I know,' he returned. 'Stagger along here. What you need is a little exercise. Step along with me.' One arm was around her waist, binding their two bodies together. What I need, she told herself grimly, is a lot more hugging and a lot less conversation. I could possibly put up with one of those patented kisses, too. How do you get a man to kiss you? I wish I knew. I wonder why Miriam never said—or even if she knew. Maybe that's why daughters get in so much trouble. They have mothers who never had to find out how to do such things.

The idea brought a little smile to her lips. 'That's better,' he commented. 'Once more up and down the beach, and then into the boat. Right?'

'Right,' she sighed. It wasn't what she wanted to hear, but obviously that was all she was going to get. And why not? she told herself as she climbed clumsily over the gunwale of the boat. He's probably known five hundred beautiful women, among whom Marcie

Waters would never be included. The idea caught up
with her as she balanced between the thwarts, and he
wasn't looking. He leaned into the stern of the craft
and pushed it off the sand. The sudden movement sent
Marcie down and back, landing with a resounding
thump on a portion of her anatomy which had already
suffered enough. There were little tears in her eyes as
she faced the bow and strangled the groan that was
forming.

The guide-boat fled through the water under John's
stroke. He was facing the stern, she the bow. A curl of
dark blue water formed, sporting a bit of lacy foam at
its peak. John hummed a tune as he worked. She
studied the curve of the lake as they moved along. A
hunting hawk stooped at the surface in front of her,
missed, and went off, disgruntled. She chuckled at the
bird's obvious chagrin. The pile of collapsed yellow in
front of her caught her eye, and she stirred it with her
foot.

My boat, she thought. My ever-loving, faithless
little boat. Such a short time from launching to
sinking. A new record? I can hardly spare it, but I
mean to go back to Sears and give them one or two
pieces of my mind! Her foot turned over another loose
segment. Her mind boggled. A piece of metal glared at
her in the light of the morning sun: a commonplace
household item, which certainly hadn't been there
when she launched the craft.

A sudden chill settled on her shoulders, weighing
her down. Her smile faded, to be replaced by a bitter
look. Someone, somehow——It could hardly be an
accident. She shrugged into herself, trying to fight off
the gloom that was gnawing at body and soul. Up and
down, that was all their relationship had been. Up and
down. John and I. Except that there isn't any John,
and there doesn't seem to be any relationship. What

kind of a game are the three of them playing with me? She bit her lip. Almost—almost he had me again. Almost, those beautiful eyes, those strong hands, that 'I've rescued the fair maiden' bit. Yeah!

'You OK?' grunted John as they came around the last bend and the house appeared.

'Yes,' she returned. A very chilly 'yes', and nothing more. He started to say something else, and then thought better of it. They approached the little wharf in silence. Only the quiet drip of water as he raised the oars and dipped them. Nobody waited. He backed the oars and nestled them against the tyre-protected pontoon.

Marcie was out of the boat as fast as her muscles could take her. Setting no national records, of course, what with all the aches and pains jostling to be heard. John flipped her a rope. It landed at her feet with a dull thud. With her back conspicuously in his direction Marcie picked it up, threw a couple of half-hitches over one of the bollards, and stalked up to the beach. He followed a few minutes later, carrying the remnants of her boat. 'Hello the house,' he called as he came up the incline.

The house door crashed open. John's grandfather— tall, thin to the limit of emaciation, white haired— came out on to the veranda. 'I was beginning to worry about you,' the old man called. He started carefully down the stairs, leaning heavily on the handrail. Marcie froze in position. Her mind told her to run for her jeep, but her body refused all the commands. John came up behind her and dumped the remains of her boat at her feet. She hardly noticed. There was something about the look in the old man's eyes, some eagerness which escaped his efforts to mask it. His grandson no longer held his attention; only Marcie occupied him. He fumbled off the bottom step and made his way slowly across the needle-strewn sand.

'Watch your step, Gramps,' warned John from behind her. The screen door of the house crashed again. Beth Fortin, arrayed in a two-piece nothing that might just qualify as a bikini, wandered out, caught one sight of John, and hurried down the steps. The old man was within six feet of Marcie when he stopped.

'Lenora!' he called. His frailty was in his voice as well as his legs. 'Nora?' Marcie hesitated, unable to move or answer. The old man moved closer, until they were face to face. 'Nora? God, what an old fool I've been! All these years.' It was a special pleading, a sigh for forgiveness from a long-forgotten ghost. Marcie shook herself out of her temporary daze.

'Marcie,' she grated. 'Marcie Waters.'

The little blonde had caught up with them, bypassing the pair to go directly to her goal. 'John!' she cooed, seizing his arm with both hands. 'You've no idea how petrified I was. You were gone all night, alone. I worried.'

'I'll bet you did,' John returned. 'But I wasn't alone. Marcie was with me.'

The little smile disappeared. 'I don't think that's funny,' said Beth.

'I didn't mean it to be,' John said grimly. 'Let's get up to the house. We could use a cup of coffee. It's a long haul down the lake. Gramps?'

'Leave me alone, boy. Go get something if you need it. I want—there's something I need to ask of Nora.'

'It's not Nora,' sighed John. 'Her name is Marcie.'

'Who the devil is Nora, anyway?' Beth interrupted harshly.

'My mother,' Marcie told her. 'Lenora.'

'You must have loved her very much,' the old man offered.

'I never knew her,' Marcie returned bitterly. 'I don't even know what she looked like.'

'She—she looked like you,' the old man said. He wavered. His grandson was at his side instantly, propping him up with a ready hand. 'Exactly like you. You could be twins, except for the long years.'

'I think you'd better go into the house,' insisted John. The old man reached out a tentative finger and traced the curve of Marcie's cheek.

'I suppose you're right,' he answered. 'You'll come, too—Marcie?'

'I suppose so.' A sudden weariness had crept up on her again, as if hearing her mother's name had brought back all the exhaustion of the past. When she had first learned it from Miriam she had spent many a night lying awake, dreaming, crying for an image which could live only in her mind. And now, here before her, was a man who had known her mother. Known and loved her? She followed the Harley men as they went slowly up to the house. Beth Fortin tagged along behind her.

'I suppose you think you've done a great thing,' Beth hissed at her. Marcie shook her head.

'No,' she replied, 'I think I've done something very stupid. Only I just don't know what it is.'

'Well, I'd be happy to tell you,' the other woman said viciously. 'Did you have a good time, bedding my fiancé?'

'I don't suppose you'd accept a denial?'

'Of course I wouldn't, I know him too well. But let me tell you, he might wander from time to time, but he always comes back!'

'That must make you feel very proud,' Marcie managed as she reached for the screen door. 'I think you're making a mistake, though. You ought to put a sign around his neck, or get his ring for your finger.'

'Damn you!' muttered Beth, pushing her inside, then hurrying around her for the kitchen. Marcie struggled along behind, just the tiniest bit bemused by the Harleys—and their cousin.

She had no time to admire the huge living room, which occupied all of the central section of the house. A wing led off in each direction. Huge French windows let in all the available sun. The furniture was solid turn-of-the-century, with a scattering of braided rugs, and a huge fireplace. The room had a lived-in look. But before the party could disappear on her she hurried after them, coming into an equally huge kitchen. The old man was just collapsing into a captain's chair at the table. John had gone over to the propane-gas stove, and was doing something about coffee.

'Over here.' The old man smiled at her and patted the seat beside him. Marcie went reluctantly. There was something about this whole crew that bothered her.

'I have a painting in my bedroom,' he told her. 'Of your mother. We'll look at it when we've had our coffee.'

Beth took a chair on the opposite side of the table. 'How can you be sure she's who she says she is?' the woman asked maliciously. 'She just wandered in up here, made a claim, and settled in. There's a great deal more investigation needed before we accept her.'

Grandfather Harley looked up. Blue eyes, like John's, Marcie told herself. Well, not quite so dark, and filled with little gleamings of steel. Beth sidled back in her chair under the scrutiny. 'I don't need any further investigation,' he said gently. 'I'd know Nora's daughter anyplace—the same look, the same hair, even the voice is the same. But if you want to investigate further, Beth, you go right ahead. We certainly wouldn't want *you* to have any doubts.'

Snap, Marcie told herself. You can hear the end of the whip crack when he swings it. Beth seemed to agree. She squirmed, and an ugly expression disturbed her perfect features.

'Coffee—black,' John announced. He plonked a mug down in front of each of them. 'Sugar in the container, milk in the refrigerator?' Marcie waved the offers away and sipped at the heavy brew. The old man did the same. Beth stared at her mug, then got up slowly and walked to the refrigerator for the milk. John settled down on Marcie's other side. Silence.

'Well what actually——'

'We had some——' Both men were talking at the same time. John waved his hand. 'So what actually happened?' his grandfather asked. As he spoke his arm extended in Marcie's direction. Not understanding why, she placed her hand in his.

'Well, I went up the lake at twilight,' John started off. 'There wasn't a thing to be seen on the lake. Along about half past six I came across a little debris.' Marcie blushed. All he has to do is make some remark about my T-shirt and slacks, she thought, and I'll fall right through the floor. Funny that neither of the other two have said anything about me being in his shirt, and no slacks. That shows you what they expect is normal for him.

'It was a whole boat load of debris,' John continued, 'about two hundred feet off the point of Crag Island. Which gave me a little scare. I picked it all up and headed for the island, and there she was, completely exhausted.'

'Exhausted, after a two-hundred-foot swim?' Beth was at her sarcastic best. The old man looked concerned. John looked stern.

'Yes,' he continued, 'exhausted. She didn't have a lifebelt, and swimming is not Marcie's best suit. She could have drowned.'

'Oh, come on,' protested Beth, 'don't exaggerate! It couldn't have been that serious.'

'It *was* that serious,' John insisted. Marcie sipped at her coffee, while the other girl squirmed in her seat.

'Faulty boat,' Grandfather Harley concluded. 'We'll sue the pants off that company! Who sold you the boat, Marcie?'

'Sears,' she responded, coughing over the coffee.

'Not their fault,' John interrupted. 'Somebody stuck a pin in the boat.'

'How could that be?' Beth asked indignantly. 'I'll bet it was some carelessness on *her* part.' She glared at Marcie. There was no doubt whom she meant.

'Carelessness, without a doubt,' ruminated John. 'You can hardly stick a pin in your own boat like that—not a safety pin.'

'A safety pin?' His grandfather was astonished, and his face showed it. 'So a pin makes a hole. How in the world do you deduce a safety pin when all you've got is a hole?'

'No deduction,' John continued doggedly. 'A straight pin makes a single hole, and would probably have been blown out by the escaping air. I know it's a safety pin because the damn thing made two holes, and it was still fastened in the holes when I found it. Take a look.' He tossed an open safety pin on to the table top in front of them all.

All this time Marcie had been watching them, with her head swinging back and forth like a spectator at a tennis match. And all the time her anger had been building up to the point where her head was about to explode. She broke in and took over.

'The pin wasn't in the boat when I bought it,' she

said very firmly. 'And it wasn't in the boat when I pumped it up and put out into the lake. And then the two of you got me to come back. Didn't you, John! You knew darn well I didn't need a water bottle—not on a freshwater lake. So you played your little game to get me away from the boat, while your dear little buddy here stuck the pin in. Just a game, wasn't it?' She pushed her chair back from the table and stood up. 'Just a little game, I suppose, to teach the dumb city girl not to play in the wilderness. What was supposed to happen?'

'Marcie, I——' he began.

'Shut up, John Harley! I've got the floor now. What was supposed to happen? Was I supposed to go a few yards down the lake and have my boat collapse? Or did one of you really figure that if you left the pin in the hole it would leak more slowly, I'd get farther away, and you'd put an end to all this inconvenience? Because that's what I've been, John Harley—an inconvenience to you and your—your—cousin!' The words were coming out like a machine gun, loaded with all the little poisons that had been accumulating in her mind for days.

'Well, let me tell you something—all of you. I may be just a kid from the city, and I suppose I don't rate in your big upper-class legal society, but I'm not ashamed of myself, or of what I do, or of where I come from. And you people don't know me from beans. You know what? To hell with you all—and——' She ran out of words.

There was so much more she wanted to say. Like, I love you with all my heart, John Harley, but you can't have me as a sideshow to your little circus. I'd like to talk to your grandfather, and know something about my own mother. I'd like that, but not at the price you're charging. I'd——Even in her mind the words piled up behind the blockade. She glared at them all; each staring at her with a different emotion on his or her face. The old man, with some deep care behind those eyes. John, with a puzzled look, too startled by events to do whatever it was he wanted to do. And Beth, with a knowing look of triumph, like an old battle-wise cat who had taken first aim at the milk.

It was more than her nerves could stand. Marcie picked up her half-empty coffee mug and threw it against the opposite wall, letting it make her final statement. Then she spun on her heels and ran out of the house as fast as her legs could carry her. It was but the work of a moment to sweep up the clutter that was her boat and throw it in the jeep.

Inside the house the three of them were still sitting at the table. 'John?' the old man prompted.

His grandson looked up from where he had been examining his own fingers, twisting them to match the concentrated lines of thought on his forehead. 'Gramps,' he said, 'if I could think of anything—anything—to prevent what just happened, I would have given all I have to do so.'

'Come on, John,' the lovely little blonde coaxed. 'She's not worth the bother. Now that she's gone we can settle back and enjoy what's left of our vacation.'

'Beth,' said John firmly, 'we've grown up together, you and I. If it wasn't for that I'd—— There were only two of us who could have stuck that pin in that boat. I didn't do it. Marcie almost drowned out there. If she had——'

His grandfather's hand dropped on John's forearm, holding him down. 'What are you going to do next?' he asked.

John looked up at him, making no effort to hide the bitterness. 'You remember that old game boys used to play?' he said. 'The one called King of the Hill?'

The old man smiled. 'The one where a kid stands on top of a mound and dares anybody to knock him off?'

'Well, when I get a few things straight around here, I'm going up that damn hill to play the game.' John pushed back his chair and strode out of the room, his face dark-hued, his eyes mirroring pain of terrible depth.

'Elizabeth,' the old man told her, staring across the table with a flinty expression, 'I think you'd better pack up and get out of here. Don't take more than an hour.'

CHAPTER EIGHT

MARCIE made sure that she wouldn't see him again. For the next four days she was up with the sun, packed her lunch and her painting materials, and went down the mountain looking for scenes to be conquered by brush-strokes. The work kept her away until five or six at night, when the best light had long since gone, and she was sure he would be busy with his grandfather. It did nothing much for her bruised feelings, but even she had to admit it had a salutary effect on her art. For the first time since coming to the Adirondacks she was showing emotion behind her brush-strokes. Her mountains were no longer pretty little pictures, but rather visual stories of earth-strengths and sky angers. Her depiction of Indian Falls drew 'oohs' from the watching crowds, and, perversely, made her feel worse. She stopped off on the way home, in Tapper Lake, and collected two pounds of home-made fudge from the Woodshed to use as a soothing balm.

'I don't know what good it would do to be rich and famous,' she told herself that fourth evening. 'It doesn't make me any happier.' She knew what *that* would take, but her pride would not let her dwell on it. Instead she made supper out of leftovers. At least the work outside would help keep her mind occupied.

With more than a little care, some advice from a friendly mechanic down in Cranberry Lake, and a book of directions, she had learned how to make the bulldozer behave. Well, *almost*. The flower garden was taking shape under this new assault. She had carefully carved a section of dirt off the side of the hill without knocking the house down, had spread it out to a depth of almost two feet, and then used her old friend, manual labour, to gather rocks for a boundary.

It was late that night, almost in darkness, that it happened. She had jockeyed the bulldozer over to the farthest corner of her new 'plantation' and was sitting there admiring her work when something slipped. At least that was what it felt like, sitting in the cab while the little engine shook her seat back and forth. One of the levers jumped.

Without her thinking about it her hand came forward to restore the control to a neutral position, and as she did so something caught the corner of her eye. It looked like that bear again, and she was in no mood for exchanging further acquaintances. Her tiny shriek of alarm was masked by a grating noise as her hand moved the lever too far. The little machine rumbled and rattled, then suddenly started backwards, and she had not yet come to the page in the instruction book about stopping runaway bulldozers.

The bear, if it were a bear, stared at the scene, marked it down to human foibles, and wandered off at a tangent into the woods. Marcie, transformed into a rusted 'tin man', sat in the saddle-seat, both hands on the offending lever, muttering, 'Oh God,' over and over as the little monster slowly backed away from the house in the general direction of the spring. One back wheel was already up over the ledge of the pool before she could muster her senses.

Both wheels were in the water before she prodded, yelled, yanked, and found a lever that would do something other than reverse. The machine grunted to a halt. The backhoe, poised like a scorpion's tail, began a wild swing to the right, and before she could do anything else but stare, its solid steel jaws slammed into the granite stone that supported the arch over the output of the spring. Satisfied with its work, the bulldozer promptly stalled.

Frightened out of her wits, Marcie did a quick survey. The back wheels of the dozer were in four feet of water; the front wheels were still up on the dry incline of the pool; the bulldozer blade in front was down; the huge jaw of the backhoe rested against the pedestal stone. And that worthy was rocking back and forth, seemingly gaining more momentum with every little swing. 'Oh, my God!' Marcie screamed.

It almost seemed that the world was waiting for that cue. The pedestal support rocked forward one more time, the arch groaned as chips flaked away from it under pressure, and the huge keystone, deprived of support, dropped straight down. It smashed into the outlet channel with a mighty crash that shook the mountain top. There was a moment of confused forest noises, then dust settled and quiet returned. Marcie Waters was left sitting on the bucket seat of her machine, looking out at the side of the mountain where water no longer dashed and trilled and fell. The keystone had completely blocked the outlet of the spring. The waterfall, which was the source of the creek, and fed the lake down there somewhere in the darkness, was as dry as if someone had turned off the tap.

'Dear heaven,' she muttered to herself, looking around in the gathering gloom. She was completely flustered. 'Five thousand gallons a day!' That was the figure the lawyers had given her. Five thousand gallons a day, this spring produced. The natural basin was wide and deep and immense. Normally, because of the steady drainage over the falls, the huge pool was only half full. But now, with its exit blocked, what? There didn't seem to be any great increase in the water level. Not yet.

She struggled with the figures. Maths had never been her best subject, but she was not totally incompetent. Five thousand gallons a day was too much to think about. Divide by twenty-four? Two hundred and eight and one-third gallons per hour. More manageable, but still too big. Divide by sixty. Three and a half gallons per minute. Well, that was a figure that didn't boggle the mind. She rolled it over on her tongue for satisfaction. Three and a half gallons— not something to worry about. Go to bed, Marcie, and things will look better in the morning!

As indeed things did. She was up at eight o'clock, fighting off the feeling that she really ought to run outside and estimate the damage. 'Don't do it,' she told the frying pan as she cracked two eggs. 'You don't really want to know, it will spoil your breakfast.' So she forced herself through the whole drill. Smile as you bite, chew everything well, take time to sip your coffee. Ruminate when the feast is over. And only then, when you can't think of another single excuse, do you throw on a pair of slacks, a blouse, brush your hair, fix your—lipstick? Isn't that overdoing it a little, fixing your lipstick before you go out to view the catastrophe? And that goes for mascara too, you nut! Her hand reluctantly returned the beauty aids to the top of the bureau, and hesitant feet carried her out into the sunshine.

Beautiful sunshine, fresh cool clean air. I'll be too spoiled to ever go back to Queens to live, she thought as she stretched. One quick peep over her shoulder. From this distance all she could really see was the kerb that ran around the pool. It was dry; no gushers of water splashed over and threatened the house. The top of the little bulldozer, forlorn, compelled her. She took a deep breath and walked slowly over in that direction.

It was pleasantly surprising. The huge pool, although considerably more full than the night before, was still not up to capacity. The air tasted as if she hadn't inhaled for hours. Which was ridiculous, she told herself sceptically. Wasn't it? The water still bubbled in the middle of the spring, the birds still chattered in the wood. Only the poor little bulldozer seemed out of place. The water level was up above the back wheels this morning, and was lapping at the brackets of the front wheels.

That's one job I need to do, get it out. And the second is that I—— His house! I get the water for my house directly from the spring. The pipe is buried underground from here to the house, then comes up over the rim and is fastened somehow to the bottom of the pool. But the water for his house——She could almost hear him saying it. 'Where your waterfall lands there's another deep pool. Our water is piped into the house directly from that area. And farther down, where it becomes a stream, we have a dam, behind which we raise small-mouth bass, for stocking the lake.' Where the waterfall lands! Marcie shook her head in panic as she walked around the circumference of the pool. Where the waterfall used to run. Bone dry now, after being shut off for over twelve hours. No waterfall. No pool? No fish? 'Oh God,' she moaned. 'If he wasn't boiling angry with me before this, how about now?'

She spun around frantically, wringing her hands. All her logic had disappeared in the face of this immense catastrophe. *Why in the world did Uncle Jack build that crazy arch? Why did I run into the stupid thing?* What if he comes up the hill—er—mountain, looking for some kind of vengeance? How soon will that pool at the foot of the waterfall get so low that he notices? Do I need someplace to hide? God help me,

I'm running hysterical again! Three and a half gallons a minute. I've got a——

What she had, after much fumbling around in the kitchen cupboard, was a five-gallon galvanised bucket. She grabbed at its handle and ran for the spring again. Her mind was completely immersed in John Harley—and three and a half gallons a minute.

She banged her knee on the frame of the bulldozer as she scrambled by it, and scraped the back of her hand on the big rock that had been the keystone of the arch. The water was deepest on the inside of the blockade. Marcie managed to get her feet spread safely, dropped her bucket in, and emptied it over the side, over the dry waterfall. The falling water sprayed and sparkled satisfactorily, and her weary mind saw success. Five gallons per bucket. At every bucketful I gain a gallon and a half—every bucket! She put her back to it. The water weight strained her muscles; there is nothing about painting that equips one for baling out a spring. She kept at it until she was panting for breath, and her wristwatch indicated fifteen minutes had passed. She stopped short. Fifteen minutes, and eight buckets full of water. A losing game!

She dropped the bucket with a groan, and settled down on the wet surface of the rocks. What I need, she told herself remorsefully, is a good cry. But the tears would not come. And I suppose I should be grateful for that, she stormed. That would mean just so much *more* water to account for! Disgustedly, she swung her legs over the inner side of the stone barrier, slipped off her sandals, and dabbled her feet in the refreshing coolness. Think!

Think about what? About John, with that lovely bronze hair, those warm blue eyes? Think about John and how wonderful it was in his arms, and how much he wanted you—before all this trouble. And how much you wanted him. What a laugh—I'm saving myself for my future husband. If he had laid one little finger more on me, the balloon would have gone up right then. And then maybe he would have loved me? Or maybe he would have enjoyed himself, marked it off as a fine one-night stand, and gone looking for some good-looking chick. Why am I so gloomy? It would have been a wonderful experience for me too, one I'd probably still be remembering on my ninetieth birthday. Because there wouldn't have been any others in between. When you've had the best, who wants the rest!

There's only one good solution, she sighed finally. Pack up my gear, load up my jeep, and go back to being the daughter of the Habib family. They'll all welcome me, and Miriam would surround me, and Hafez would absorb me in love.

I could write to Mr Vanderpol, the lawyer, and tell him that it was all a mistake. That I wasn't the right Marcie Waters. He'd have to go on searching for somebody else. If I did it all well, I could fall back into obscurity in my own little neighbourhood, and maybe marry the boy next door and raise half a dozen Lebanese kids. That's a 'live happily ever after' ending, so how come *now* I'm crying?

She noticed something else, too. Although the top part of her was wet with tears, the lower part was *not* wet with spring water. Not any more. She managed to clear one eye with a dirty knuckle and looked down. The level of water in the pool was receding, much faster than it had formerly risen! Marcie jumped to her feet with a little screech. No, it wasn't flowing down the slight incline towards her house, and no, it wasn't falling happily down its old waterfall path. But it was receding.

'And who cares where it's going?' she chortled in wild abandon. 'Everything's OK again!' She gave one more shout of joy, and danced back towards the house. A flock of starlings, alarmed by the noise, scattered from their roost under the birch trees, raucously maligned her as they swept overhead, and moved on.

'Well,' she announced to the world, 'you certainly solved *that* problem, Marcie. Now how about rescuing the bulldozer?'

Nothing seemed impossible. Blue skies, clear seeing, great problem-solving. And it was only a small bulldozer at that! She wandered over to her jeep. Under the back seat was a six-foot towing chain. It had come with the vehicle when she purchased it third-hand, and had never before now been disturbed. She hummed a little song as she worked.

The chain was heavier than she had expected; six feet of case-hardened steel was not something to be taken casually. She put her back into it. Funny, that. All the moaning and groaning she had done as a child under Miriam's thumb in the kitchen. 'I'm nothing but a slave—that's what!' And the laughter *that* had brought. 'You don't know what slaving is,' Miriam had chided. 'Wait until you're grown up!'

And here she was, grown up, doing her best to shift six feet of heavy steel chain. By dint of a great deal of tugging and towing and growling the chain was moved. There was a tow-hook just above the bulldozer blade, and the chain slipped on as if meant for it. The jeep was a little more trouble. Marcie backed it around carefully, but had to hump up over the lip of the pool and down into almost two feet of water before the connection could be made. But at last it was. She inspected the job carefully, then took a quick look at the sun, directly overhead. Noontime, her stomach clock told her. Time for lunch.

Marcie found it hard to prepare a meal just for herself. The past weeks had spoiled her for that. It was with a false sense of gaiety that she produced a ham salad, and sat down to dispose of it. Something was troubling her mind, and she could not identify it. She felt like the man in the story, she told herself. The man with the sword hanging over his head. Damocles? The salad tasted good, and was one of her favourites, but not for today. Eventually, having managed four or five bites, she covered the plate with plastic wrap and shoved it into the refrigerator.

Still haunted by that feeling, she forced herself to go back outside. 'To the scene of the crime,' she teased herself and, instead of laughing, managed another tear or two. Sitting disconsolately in the driver's seat of the jeep, she wavered again. How simple it would be if only John were here. Maybe it *is* chauvinism—the female sort—but how much nicer it would be if he were sitting where I am, and I could stand off to one side and cheer him on while he restored everything to what it once was. That 'everything' to include a spare kiss or two, and a retreat to before Beth Fortin had arrived on the scene. And then, after he had retrieved all the equipment and set the spring to rights, well then, if he should happen to follow her into her bedroom, should they just happen to fall down on her bed again—lord, it would be a different ending, Marcie Waters!

Her hand reached for the ignition key. The old jeep bucked and rattled a time or two, and then settled down into a sedate puttering. She took one more look backward at her arrangement of chains, then to the side, where the water level seemed to have established a new and lower mark. Everything appeared to be all right. Her foot moved to the clutch, and she pushed in the four-wheel-drive.

She eased out the clutch very gently. The jeep chattered and groaned, the steel chain went taut, but nothing else happened. Marcie shook her head in disgust. The brakes on the bulldozer, of course. She had set them almost automatically when she climbed out earlier in the day.

She climbed out of the jeep, leaving the motor warming up, and waded back to the bulldozer. It took but a moment to release the brakes. She checked the chain again. It looked properly attached. The bulldozer blade bothered her, though it was down, resting with one corner on the rock of the pool, it could only be raised with the engine of the bulldozer running, and *that* engine was underwater. She shrugged her shoulders. What can't be cured must be endured. Another one of Miriam's old Arabic sayings, translated from the old English, or maybe even some language earlier than that? The idea lightened her gloom. She was giggling as she waded back to the jeep and climbed in.

The engine rumbled satisfactorily. There was nothing to block the mission. Her foot went to the pedal, hand moved the gear shift, and once again she let the clutch in gently. The vehicle bucked and the back wheels spun. She pushed down on the accelerator. Something moved, but not straight ahead. Sideways.

Marcie watched with fear in her eyes as the jeep gradually slipped and slid sideways, tethered by an immovable object, into deeper water. Her hands were wrapped around the useless steering wheel in a death-lock. Her foot was pressed down hard on the accelerator, and nothing she could do would remove it. The wheels spun, splashing up waves of water into and around the jeep. The sideways movement became more acute. Water flowed over the low sill of the door at her side. The engine gave two or three bronchial coughs, and stopped. Everything was quiet. Not even the blue jays dared to offer an opinion. Marcie sat in the seat, hands still glued to the wheel, water up to her waist, stunned.

It seemed to be hours, but was perhaps only minutes, before she heard another engine. Her eyes almost refused her command to look. They were glued on the water, the cold clear water, but eventually they shifted their focus just as the truck came up slowly over the crest of the hill, and drove on up to the house. His truck, of course. John.

She watched as he climbed out and walked around the front of the vehicle. Even at a distance she could see he was angry. He walked with a stiff-legged stride that was easily readable. And for some reason Marcie could not find the strength to move. She sat there in the jeep and watched the water eddy around her. Watched John as he carefully opened the other door of the truck and helped his grandfather out. Watched as John took one long look in her direction and then ignored her.

Grandfather Harley rested an arm on John's shoulder as he moved. He seemed to be tired. Marcie could not hear a word of their conversation, but one of them was laughing. The pair struggled up the steps to her front porch, and went into the house. A few minutes later John came back out, reached into the back of the truck, and pulled out four suitcases. Either the suitcases or the back of the truck was wet—it was hard to tell at this distance, and Marcie was feeling too miserable to give it much thought. John disappeared into the house again.

What are they doing in my house? she asked herself. Not angrily, or with emotion, because her emotions were all used up. Just curious. What I ought to do is get out of this darn jeep and stomp in there and demand to know! But I just don't have the strength, do I? What I ought to do at least is get up and get out of this—this lake. But even that was beyond her. So she just sat there, hunched over the useless steering wheel, her misery and pain plain to see as the chill of the water brought on uncontrollable shivers. John came out of the house again. He stood on the porch and looked all around, then casually strolled over towards the spring. He stopped again at the lip of the pool hands on hips, legs spread slightly apart to brace himself. Staring.

She was beginning to work her way up out of apathy. If he laughs I'll kill him, she promised. Just one little titter. He didn't. His carved face reflected not the slightest bit of humour. He moved down slowly into the water and waded over to the jeep.

'Go ahead, say it!' she snarled.

'Oh? Say what?'

'Some crack about woman drivers.'

'Oh, that. Some mess you've got here.'

'I didn't invite you to come and look. If it insults your aesthetic tastes, I won't try to keep you. I didn't invite you!' Anger was just what she needed. Her blood began to stir. Or maybe it wasn't *all* anger. He was standing so close, and looked so—so edible.

'You did it on purpose, didn't you?' he said. 'Just what was it you were trying to prove?'

'You wouldn't believe it if I told you,' she answered gloomily. And then, more sharply, 'What do you mean about me trying to prove something?'

'Looks as if the bulldozer is really stuck. I suppose the outlet is blocked?'

'I——' Marcie licked her dry lips. All of a sudden they had arrived at the moment of truth. He didn't actually sound angry. In fact, she had never heard him talk so calmly, so casually. Usually every other one of his words sparkled with humour, and that's one reason why I love him, she told herself. But not now. Straightforward, calm, but not uninterested. Certainly not that. A little chill of panic ran up her spine. He's up to something, her mind screamed. He acts like a volcano that's going to erupt tomorrow!

'Yes,' she sighed, 'I guess you could say the outlet is blocked. The arch—the stone—I—— Why did Uncle Jack put it up there in the first place?'

He cleared his throat and shifted his weight. 'I told you once before. He wanted to cover the pool to keep out bird droppings. I used to think he was crazy, but compared to you he seems now to have been perfectly normal. Did you have to go to all this trouble just to get even with the Harley family? I can't figure out whether you're an evil genius, or just operating with only three wheels. Well, if you meant to drive us out of house and home, lady, you've done it to perfection. And since you've done us in, we're going to camp out up here for the remainder of our vacation. Lord! Crazy!'

A flicker of rebellion struggled to the surface of her mind. She fought to her feet, standing on the seat of the jeep. The water was only up to her ankles, and ran down off her in cascades, which only added to the conflagration. 'Don't you say that,' she snapped. 'Don't you dare talk about—about—don't you dare!'

'Don't I dare?' There was no laughter at all in him. 'After this fiasco, don't I dare? Why, you flaming idiot! Have you any idea what you've done?' He leaned over into the jeep, too close for comfort. She wanted to run, all the way back to the little house in Queens, but instead, her right hand came round with all the force she could put into it and slapped his face with a resounding thud that startled both of them.

John might not have been particularly hurt, but the

blow did catch him off balance. His foot slipped. He made a wild grab for the roll-bar on the jeep and missed. Marcie watched aghast as he teetered and then fell over backwards into the water.

'Oh hell!' she muttered. The tears were forming in her eyes, and her hand smarted as if all the bones had been broken. He came to the surface spluttering, climbed to his feet, and glared at her. With the water cascading down off *his* frame things looked a little different. She was unable to suppress the hysterical laughter. It shook her stomach, rolled drily out of her parched throat, and echoed off the mountain.

'I don't see anything funny about that,' he spluttered, wiping his face with one huge hand. Marcie was truly caught, and could not stop. 'Must be funny as hell,' muttered John as he moved towards her. She heard the words distantly as he picked her up. His shirt-front was cold and wet, and still she could not stop laughing, until she looked to see where he was carrying her. They were working their way deeper into the pool, and the water was up to his waist, wetting the bottom of her slacks.

'Wait!' she shrieked.

'Funny,' he muttered as he heaved her out ahead of him close to the maelstrom that was the centre of the spring. She hit the water with a tremendous splash, and was immediately drawn into the whirling fountain at the centre of the spring. Just the simple physical act had already released his tensions, his angers. He watched grimly to mark the place where she would come up. I'll scare the hell out of her, he told himself, then forget all the angers, and take up where we left off a few days ago. But she didn't come up. He watched impatiently, and then fearfully. A picture flashed through his mind: Marcie on the island, exhausted, after swimming hardly two hundred feet.

'You damn fool!' he reviled himself, and dived deep
into the clear blue water.

Despite the clarity of the water it was hard to see
anything because of the turmoil. John forced himself
directly up to the water-spout, then circled around it,
without any luck. A quick surfacing for a deep breath,
and he went down again, searching aimlessly. When
he came up the second time he was beginning to feel
the doubts, the worries—and his conscience was
heavier than his logging boots. He broke free, forced
himself up as high as possible, and made a quick
search of the horizon. There was a shadow clinging to
the bright yellow of the bulldozer. Fear drove his arms
in a battering crawl stroke, full speed, until his
outstretched right arm touched the metal of the
machine, and his left found a soft something. He lifted
his head and shook the hair out of his eyes. Marcie was
clinging to the cab of the dozer with both hands, eyes
squeezed shut, shivering.

'All right, all right,' he soothed as he hooked a leg in
the machinery and gathered her up. At his touch her
arms abandoned the cold welcome of the steel and
fumbled for his shoulders, his throat, the nape of his
neck, and tightened for dear life. 'All right,' he
muttered in her ear. He used one hand to guide them
around the machinery and out on to the rock surface of
the retaining wall. The other hand pressed against her
back, trying to soothe, to calm, to reassure.

'It's all over, love,' he said, as soon as his free hand
found a purchase on the rocks. 'Up you go now.' He
tried to set her up on top of the parapet, but her hands
would not unlock from around his neck. She was
moaning wordlessly. With a tremendous surge of
strength he managed to push them both up and out of
the pool, and still her hands held. John cherished her
with his hands, used the time to regain his breath, and

then stood up, holding her gently in his arms.

They were both soaked and chilled, but she cuddled up against his chest as if it were a warm dry refuge. He walked carefully, balancing himself on the lip of the pool as they circled around it and out on to dry land. He stopped to readjust her weight, and one of her eyes opened. 'Are you angry with me?'

'Yes,' he announced. 'You're all right now.'

'I know,' she sighed, snuggling closer. 'You're really angry with me.' A doleful statement, not a question.

'Yes, really. It takes some kind of guts to fall in love with a crazy like you,' he sighed.

'Have you—— Do you——' Weakly, hesitantly, as if her lips would not willingly form the words, 'Have you got that kind?'

'You'd better believe it!' John shifted her weight again and started off for the house.

CHAPTER NINE

MARCIE relaxed completely, as a little girl would when her world falls in on her and a father's arms are offered. It was a total withdrawal from pain, from problems, from worries, leaving all that minor material in the hands of one much stronger. Despite his sternness, there seemed to be a twitch of happiness at the corners of his mouth as he looked at her cold wet face. Or maybe I'm kidding myself, she thought. I can't seem to stop shaking!

His grandfather was waiting for them, holding the screen door open. As John squeezed by, the old man touched one of her hands and noticed her shaking. 'Right into the hot shower, boy,' he said gruffly. 'She's in shock. Get her warmed up on the outside. I'll fumble around in the kitchen and see if I can concoct some hot soup.'

John might have spoken, but Marcie was too deep in here daze to catch what was said. She remembered the trip down the corridor. Her head lolled from side to side, her long wet hair trailing behind them. He slammed the bathroom door behind them with the heel of his boot, then stood her up on the bathmat. Her feeble feet wobbled and she fell against him, clutching for his neck. It seemed impossible to quell the shaking. She struggled against it, only managing to work up a tear.

His hands were busy, stripping off all her soaked clothing. She clung all the tighter. John used one hand to support her back, and the other to turn on the hot water. In seconds steam was pouring out, flooding the bathroom with warmth. He let it run for a minute or two, then adjusted the cold water tap.

'All right now, Marcie,' he ordered, 'in you go.' He picked her up as if she weighed nothing, and stood her in the shower under the warm spray. When his hands disappeared she wobbled, and almost fell. 'Oh, hell!' he grunted. With only one eye open she watched as he kicked off his boots and pulled off his shirt. She reached out towards him, and suddenly he was in the shower with her, pulling her up against his solid chest. 'Better?'

'Yes,' she whispered, struggling to get closer. The warmth was gradually penetrating. Her shaky limbs were slowly returning to normal, but she was not about to give up the support he offered. Her mind was gradually resuming control of her body. And what about you, her conscience teased, standing naked in a shower with a grown man? She turned her head to one side, nestling it in the wiry cushion of hair on his chest. Bronze, she noted, just like on his head. That's unusual, isn't it? She really didn't know. She had seen a thousand men or more on Jones Beach, stripped to the waist, and never noticed. Her arms were tiring. She released her death-grip, flexed her arms, then wrapped them around his torso. It was a full stretch, that, and her arms were not long enough to reach all the way around. But it was nice.

'Hey, don't go to sleep on me!' John's mouth was just at her ear. Both his hands, covered with soap lather, were massaging her back. They moved in wide circles from her rounded hips to her tired shoulders, gently, while she gloried in the feeling. He turned her around, so her back was against his stomach, and continued the massage across her stomach, down over her flat belly, up over her risen breasts. And all the time the warm water worked on her chill. The need to sleep was being offset by other needs, ones of which she had no prior experience. She shuddered. His hands stopped, and he turned her around to face him, holding her about a foot away. Her body struggled to make contact again; her mind just watched.

'Warmer?'

'Mmm,' she managed to get out. She tried again to close the gap between them.

'Want your hair shampooed?'

Little warning bells started to ring in Marcie's mind. John's hands kept her at a distance despite her troubles, and the bells grew louder. They could not be ignored. 'No,' she sighed. 'I've got you all wet, haven't I?'

It almost seemed that he hadn't noticed. At her comment he looked down at his soaked trousers and chuckled. 'It's better than being out in that spring, lady. OK, that's enough for now. He urged her out on to the bathmat and enveloped her with one of the massive towels from the rack. She wound it around her and tucked it in. 'Bow your head,' he ordered. She complied.

He held a smaller towel in both hands, and used it now to rub-dry her hair. He didn't seem to know his own strength; Marcie had to spread her feet and brace herself to keep from being knocked over. 'Any complaints?' he asked as he kept busily at it.

Complaints? she thought. Even a fool like me

knows when she's well off! You won't find *me* complaining, mister. Rub away. I don't care if you rub it all off! But when his fingers caught in one of the tangles, her inadvertent yelp brought it all to an end. John handed her another towel.

'Out in the kitchen,' he ordered. 'It'll be warmer out there, and Gramps will have something hot for you to drink.' He gave her a small, gentle shove towards the door.

'You're not coming?' She gave an inarticulate moan.

'I'll be along,' he chuckled, urging her on with a pat on her bottom.,

'But I——' Marcie swallowed her complaint and ran as he started to unzip his soaked trousers.

Grandfather Harley was sitting at the kitchen table when she ran in. She stopped short. The old man was resting his head on the palm of one hand, looking as if he was exhausted. It was her first real chance to study him. He and his grandson would make a pair of matched bookends, she told herself. The old man is frail and a lot thinner, but it's plain to see that when he was younger he must have been a prize! His bushy hair is completely white, but there's such a lot of it. His eyes are a paler blue than John's, and his skin sports one or two liver spots. But altogether, still a fine figure of a man! She cleared her throat and he looked up.

'Ah, Marcie. Sit down, my dear. You look a million miles better.'

'I'll bet I do,' she laughed, as she settled into the chair opposite him. 'I feel as if I've been dragged through a hedge backwards!'

'On you anything would look good,' he contributed.

He unfolded from the table and went over to the stove. 'All I could find was mugs for the soup. I hope you're not too proud to eat canned soup?'

'Not me,' she laughed, cupping the proffered mug between her hands. 'I'm a Campbells soup girl myself.' She sipped tentatively at the hot drink. And then, 'You said you knew my mother?'

'Very well,' the old man returned. His eyes seemed to light up, as if he were returning to a favourite subject. 'Your mother was the little girl down the block when we were all young, living in New Rochelle. She practically grew up under foot, so to speak. A lovely lady, Lenora. She looked—— You're almost a spitting image of her, Marcie. You startled me when I first saw you the other day. Oh, I know that my grandson thinks I'm getting senile.' He lifted up one hand to stem her protests. 'And who knows, maybe I am, but I remember Lenora. A wonderful, lovable girl. And you could have been my granddaughter.'

'Is that why you and my Uncle Jack—you had a fight about my mother?'

'Not exactly,' he sighed. 'We were good friends, your great-uncle and I. Business partners, too. But when that—that nephew of his—— Damn! I can't even think about that man after all these years without getting mad.'

'My father?'

'Yes, your father. He poisoned things between our two families, plucked Lenora away from us, and just disappeared. I'm sorry to have to tell you, but it's true—he was a rotten man. He married your mother out of spite, not out of love. And we never did hear from either of them again. None of us knew, Marcie, that you even existed. I'm sorry.'

'You needn't be on my account,' she told him. 'I never knew him. I never knew her.'

'You poor kid! And you know the worst part about it? In spite of all his boasting, he was one lousy painter, believe me.'

'So.' Marcie stopped to consider. 'So that's where I got it from,' she continued. 'And I might just turn out to be a lousy painter too.' There was a chuckle behind her words. He returned the smile.

'I doubt it,' he said, 'not if that scene out on your easel is your work. It's loaded with feelings, Marcie. That's what a painting ought to reveal: feelings.'

And what can you say to that? she asked herself, as she finished off the soup. I think it's well done myself! And aren't I the little modesty girl?

'But I don't want you to feel sorry for me,' she went on determinedly. 'I'm one of those orphans who lucked out. I have a fine Lebanese mother, and a wonderful Lebanese father, and they had two boys besides. I never even knew I was an orphan until the lawyers came to see me.'

'Well, I won't say another word. More soup?'

Marcie accepted the offer. Old Mr Harley brought the saucepan from the stove and poured. When he was seated again she probed for what she really wanted to know. 'But when I first came, you didn't want to see me, or anything? John was building a fence across the road, and——'

'Bullheaded.' He interrupted her in mid-sentence and waved a hand. 'All Harleys tend to be that way— you'll find that out. John is just the same. Or maybe, to be truthful, I was afraid to meet you, Marcie. I've carried Nora so long in my heart that I was afraid of what I might see. When we came up the hill I noticed that the whole fence had been bulldozed?'

'I—— Yes. I lost my temper. Somebody padlocked the gate, and I couldn't get down the mountain to get food, and that made me so—I wasn't very lady-like, I guess. Do you want me to pay for the fence?'

'No, of course not. It was all a terrible idea in the first place. I really thought that the place up here would be auctioned off. I don't mind people using the road, but I didn't want it to become some common-law right of way.'

'But if you didn't care, who could have padlocked it? John?'

'I doubt it. More than likely Elizabeth. That's one very disturbed lady, Elizabeth Fortin.'

'Lawyers are disturbed?' queried Marcie. 'I thought—I didn't know.'

'There are as many crazy lawyers as there are crazy psychiatrists,' he laughed. 'And in my experience with shrinks, there are plenty of those. Now, please accept an old man's apologies, Marcie, and we'll go on from there.'

She looked deep into him, beyond his face, and discarded the melodramatic appeal. 'Why, you're really an old fraud, aren't you,' she chuckled. 'Of course I accept. And now are you going to stay with me for a time?'

'And you'd better believe that, too!' A strong deep voice, from behind her. Marcie turned around and stared. John had not only dried himself off, but had managed to find some clean clothes. And here I am dressed in a towel, she thought. Am I never going to meet this man when I have the advantage? She shifted nervously in her chair. His grandfather was smiling; John was not.

He came over to the table and sat down between them. 'Yes,' he said sternly. 'We're both going to be staying with you for a few days.'

She gulped—it was hard not to. He sounded like someone who ate nails for lunch, and topped it off with a glass of prussic acid. 'You're—you're still angry with me?'

'You could say that. It's accounting time, young lady.'

'Accounting for what?' It was difficult to get the words out. Her throat was not just dry, it was parched.

'Accounting for the water,' he said.

Oh God, she thought, I did it. The pool that feeds his house is bone dry! 'I—— Did I cut off the water from your house?' she whispered. Both the men laughed uproariously. Marcie sat at the table and stared at them in astonishment as they rocked back and forth. 'Well, if it's all that funny,' she added, 'at least you could tell me about it!'

'Oh, I intend to,' returned John as he struggled to get his breath back. 'But first, Gramps couldn't sleep last night, and he's not had a meal this morning, so you take care of that little problem, and get him settled, while I go take a look outside.'

'Yes, sir!' she snapped, then blushed. John glared at her, then scraped back his chair and left. 'Yes, I will,' she added at his retreating back. He stopped and looked over his shoulder.

'That's better,' he retorted. 'Submissive, but not too

humble. I like that.' Her mouth was still hanging open when the screen door slammed behind him.

'He's a lot of man,' his grandfather said from behind her.

She turned slowly, trying to hide the colouration. 'Yes,' she admitted. 'What would you like for lunch?'

John was gone for almost an hour, by which time Marcie had come to call the old man Gramps at his insistence, and had seen two bacon, lettuce and tomato sandwiches disappear behind those picket teeth.

'Best thing that ever happened to our family,' the old man told his grandson as he came in. 'Your mother never could cook, and your grandmother didn't even know where the kitchen was.'

'Don't count your horses too quickly,' warned John. 'I haven't even asked her yet.'

'You young people who think you know so much don't even know the time of day. Marcie, I'm going to lie down for a while. I know the room.'

'I've changed the sheets,' she said anxiously. 'Do you want me to show you the way?'

'No, I can find it,' he laughed. 'Why don't you just sit here with my not-too-bright grandson and see if you can't straighten him out?'

'And what do you suppose he meant by that?' John stomped over to the table and sat down. 'A BLT sandwich?' His grandfather had left hardly a clue on his plate. 'I could use one of those myself.'

'I——' Cooking is better than trying to explain myself, Marcie's wary mind told her. Considering that he was his grandfather's image, she made enough for three and constructed a grilled cheese for herself as she did so. His eyes were on her all the time; she could feel them boring into her back, right through the fluffy thick towel. Towel? I'm standing here dressed in nothing but a bath towel! Her fingers fumbled, and she almost dropped the plate as she tried to set it in front of him.

'Lost your cool?'

'Lost my clothes,' she gasped, and rushed to remedy the situation. It didn't take long. Not more than thirty minutes, while she slipped into jeans and a blouse. Most of the time was spent on her hair, brushing it until it crackled, and then quickly braiding and pinning everything up into a coronet. A touch of lipstick wouldn't hurt, either, her mirror image advised, and perhaps a little of that dark eye-liner, and some mascara—and don't walk out there without some perfume, you prize idiot! A touch of powder for her nose, and she was off.

John's plate was empty, and he looked as if he was too. Marcie bustled to the stove, made up the third sandwich, and presented it on a new plate. As she set this one down he trapped her wrist. 'Fee-fi-fo-fum,' he grumbled, 'I smell the blood of one lovely lady.'

'You'd better let me go,' she muttered in return. 'In addition to being fresh, you're also half blind. Turn me loose before your grandfather hears.'

'He won't hear a thing until three o'clock,' he laughed. He pulled her down into his lap. I'm not a pushover, Marcie whispered to herself over and over. I'm not one of those women of his with round heels. I won't—— But by the time she reached the second verse of the song she was singing she had forgotten all the words. His lips had closed in on her again. First a

gentle exploration, and then a massive engagement as
he took over her body, her soul, her psyche. She
struggled for perhaps as long as a tenth of a second,
then hauled down her flag and gloried in the
sensations. So much so that when John pushed her
gently away she moaned a protest, and he laughed.

The laugh was a mistake. It snapped her back out of
her daze and on to real time. 'Darn you,' she muttered
as she struggled free and stood up. Her blouse was in
disarray. She fought with the little pearl buttons.

'Want some help?'

'You—you've helped enough,' she said crossly. His
hand reached, but she ducked away from it and put
the table between them. 'I'm not on the menu, and
you'd better understand that!'

She didn't wait for an answer, but bit into her
cheese sandwich as if there was nothing more to be
said. As she munched she hoped that he wouldn't
return to *that* subject. What a strange person I must
be, she thought. I didn't mind doing it—not in the
least. I just hate talking about it. And doesn't that tell
you something?

Over the top of her own bread she watched as John's
strong teeth tore his own sandwich into shreds. He
ate—enthusiastically—that was the word that fitted.
Very polite, very neat, but enthusiastically. Miriam
popped into her mind again. Quotation: It's a pleasure
to feed someone who enjoys what you prepare. Yes, it
was. She could not repress the tiny smile. It seemed out
of place at such a solemn table, and she wiped it off
immediately. He was wiping his fingers on the paper
napkin, and looking around for something else to
gnaw on.

'Want another?' she offered. He nodded. Marcie put her own dry sandwich down and went to the stove. While her busy hands moved, she pondered. So much had been said recently that needed explanation and she didn't quite know where to start. Do you have enough guts to love someone like me? You better believe it. Lord, I could use about twenty pages of discussion on that. But it's not a safe subject. How about ——

'Why did you both laugh when I asked if I'd shut off the water in your house?' she asked.

'You really want to know?'

'Of course I do. If I—I did something wrong I want to know.'

'Most women would rather forget it,' John remarked.

'If you expect me to say I'm not most women, forget it,' she sighed. 'On second thoughts, I don't want to know.'

'But you're going to,' he threatened. He trapped her hand again in his, and pulled her over to the table.

'The bacon,' she spluttered. 'I'll—you—the bacon!'

'OK,' he chuckled. 'Hoist by my own petard, huh? So fix the bacon. I'll collect my dessert later.'

'I didn't make any dessert,' Marcie muttered as she struggled free and flicked ineffectively at her clothing.

'Yes, you did,' he chuckled. 'Now, about the water. I take it you had a good time with your bulldozer?'

She concentrated on turning the slim slices over on their other side. John liked his bacon crisp, she knew. 'I—— Yes, I had a great deal of fun,' she admitted. 'I got the garden soil spread out, and—and——'

'And?'

'And then I—something startled me, and I hit the wrong lever, and it went into reverse, and I couldn't stop it, and then we——'

'Backed into the arch?'

'Yes.' Defiantly stated. Perhaps even a little shrill. Marcie was trying desperately to keep her voice non-committal, and wasn't having a great deal of luck. 'And don't you dare say anything about women drivers! Not a word!'

'I won't.' It was a promise that rested on laughter. Concealed, of course, but noticeable to a super-sensitive woman who was looking for just such a connotation.

'And then the arch fell down, and blocked the channel and I tried to get it open and I couldn't, so I tried to bale the spring out with a bucket, and it wouldn't, and then I went to pull the bulldozer out and——'

'Whoa! Catch your breath.' She stopped on command, and stood there, her breasts heaving in magnificent storm which only he could see. 'Now, slowly,' coaxed John.

'And then——' Why were those darn tears inter-rupting! She dashed them aside with her knuckle. 'And then I put the chain on to tow the bulldozer, and it wouldn't move,'—slowly, Marcie, slowly—'and the jeep just suddenly slipped to one side, and that's when you came up the hill.' So! Two deep inhalations, and then a third. Hands clenched, down at your sides. Face flushed. Eyes stormy, and just a tiny bit wet. And what do you dare to say to that, man?

John was perhaps the wisest man she had ever met. He said not a word. And that's why I love him, she shouted at herself. He's not just a lover, but a wonderful friend. What does a woman need in a husband? Miriam again: You need a best friend who can set you on fire with a single touch—a man full of compassion who loves children.

'But it can't be all that bad,' she whispered into the silence that followed her diatribe. 'I was sitting on the stone.' Not crying—don't tell him that part; that's all he's seen of you in the past weeks. A regular watering-pot, that's what. 'I was just—sitting there. And the water went back down again. The level, I mean, in the spring. So everything's going to be all right, isn't it?'

'Yes,' he returned. 'After a bit, everything will be all right. So where do you think the water went?'

'I—I don't know. Is it important?' Busy hands. Thank heaven they don't require a brain to supervise! She finished constructing the sandwich and put it down in front of him. My, he eats a lot, she thought, but then he's a big man. If he were mine, I would have to double the weekly shopping. If he were mine. Dreamer!

'Not really,' he answered between bites. 'I'll get it fixed one way or another. But you did surprise us.'

'When the—when the water went off?'

'When the water turned on,' chuckled John. 'In case you hadn't noticed, there's a break in the retaining wall of the pool, over on the east side.'

'And that's where it's leaking out? Well, that's all right then, isn't it?'

'You're not much for geography, are you, Marcie?'

'I—perhaps not. Why?'

'Because, lady, the stream that once ran down the north side of the mountain and into the lake is now running down the east side. And what else is there over on the east side?'

Don't tell me, she pleaded. I don't want to know. But John's mouth was opening as she watched. Everything seemed to be moving in slow motion. She clapped her hands over her ears. I don't want to hear! she screamed at herself.

'There's a cove in the mountain, over on the east side,' John went on. I don't want to hear, she insisted silently. Her brain echoed with the pain of it, and he didn't notice. 'And in that cove, back up against the mountain,' he plodded on, 'is my grandfather's cabin, right?' A smile. There's nothing funny about any of this, she stormed inside her head.

'We thought it was strange, along about daybreak, when it started to rain so hard, Marcie. I got up to close the windows, and the sun was shining in. Would you believe that?'

No, I wouldn't believe that, she thought. I won't believe anything! Her hands pressed more strongly over her ears. And still he went on.

'Then after an hour or so, what do you suppose? Not only was it raining on us from a brand-new waterfall where none had ever been before, but a new stream began to trickle down the cliffs behind us, and the first thing I knew it was flowing in through the French windows in our living room, straight through Gramps's bedroom, and down the front stairs to the beach. What do you say about that?'

'Nothing,' she managed to gasp. And that's my last word on *that*, John Harley. You don't have me in a witness box, and I'm not going to submit to an inquisition. Not me! Never!

'Was Gramps—was your grandfather injured? I——'

'Well, he was considerably wetter than he wanted to be, that's for sure.'

'And you—what did you do?'

'Well, like a couple of idiots we tried to find some way to stop the flood down at our level. When that didn't work, we moved all the good furniture out of the way. And by that time we both concluded something had happened on top of the mountain.'

'So you packed up and came running?'

'What else? All I could think of was some catastrophe up here, and you lying at death's door—even Gramps was worried.'

'It wasn't because you wanted to get even or get a free meal or anything like that?'

'Nothing like that. Come over here.'

The sun took that moment to sneak out from behind a cloud. It flooded the atrium with light, diffusing through the ornamental glass prisms she had hung only a week before. Rainbow colours made a magic welcome. The world looked brighter, felt happier. John was holding out both hands. She went willingly.

The hands were gentle on her tall frame. It was not submission, but rather a sharing. He tugged her gently down on to his lap, hugged her close, and rubbed a cheek across her soft burnished hair. 'Some day real soon I need to ask you something,' he whispered.

'OK,' she whispered back.

'Me too.' She was so startled that she actually jumped. Gramps was standing in the door, laughing at them both. 'I——' Her hand fumbled at her blouse, which was not, for once, at all in disarray. 'You—you want something?' she asked. 'I thought you would nap longer. John said—he——'

'Has that rascally grandson of mine been talking out of turn again?' the old man asked. 'You'd think that as a lawyer he would know better. I hate to interrupt at what might be an important time, but it seems more propitious to remind you both of something.'

John got up, and Marcie studied him as he moved. His face was under control again. For just a moment, before the interruption, she had seen that he was in as much of a turmoil as she was, but now he was back in charge again. 'What is it, Gramps?' No sound or word of censure. No anger. A straightforward concern for the older man, expressed in a level-headed manner.

'First,' the old man chuckled, 'there's the problem about where we're going to eat and sleep tonight. It's still not too late for us to get on the road. We could be back in my Manhattan apartment by dinner time at the latest.'

'Do you want to go, Gramps?'

'What, and miss the best of the fun? I haven't had as nice a day as this in years.'

'In spite of the water and all?'

'Because of the water and all. Well?'

'If you would both like to stay, I would love to have you,' Marcie invited. 'It would be a shame for you to miss your last few days of vacation. And I'd be honoured to make your meals, sir.'

'Ah,' the old man chuckled. He came all the way into the kitchen. 'Well said. But how about the boy?'

Marcie was caught short, and had to fumble. It was just impossible for her to think of John as 'the boy'. Evidently he thought she was delaying for some other reason. He looked at her quickly, and his smile disappeared. Hurry, her mind screamed, say something, even if it's wrong!

'John too,' she stuttered. 'I—you surprised me. I can't quite think of John as—I thought there might be someone else.'

They both roared, a full-throated masculine seal of approval. Her heart resumed beating. The smile was back on John's lips. He caught her up in a warm bearhug that rattled her ribs and didn't do a great deal for her peace of mind, either.

'Now that the important part is decided,' Grandfather Harley commented, 'we'd better not forget the secondary. If that new stream continues running through our house for very long the foundations are going to be washed away. We have "builded our house on sand", boy, and must pay the penalty, as the Good Book says. Unless your clever mind can think up some quick solution?'

'My first thought was to let the whole thing wash out to sea,' chuckled John. 'But I can see I'd be outvoted.'

'And what the devil would you be doing while it did?' The two of them were using the rapier. The conversation was too far over Marcie's head. She shrugged, and turned towards the food cupboards.

'That's for me to know, and you to guess,' his grandson answered. Marcie's cheeks flushed red as a rose. It was going to take some fancy footwork, she told herself, to keep up with these two. But you want to, her mind told her. You want to, so stop blathering about things, and get on with your part of the job!

CHAPTER TEN

'IT'S a lead-pipe cinch,' John told his grandfather some hours later. 'All we really need is a couple of sticks of dynamite.'

'Watch that,' the old man said. 'You're a lawyer. Just because you had a demolition course when you were drafted in the army it doesn't make you an expert. There's some old saying about cobblers sticking to their last—you've heard that?'

'Oh, Gramps!' laughed John. 'For a man who's respected for his command of English, you're falling deeper and deeper into the cliché trap! It's simple. There's only one boulder blocking the old exit. We don't even have to split the rock, just move it a few feet. And even I can do that. Can't I, Marcie?'

'Of course,' she heard herself agreeing. Of course what? I haven't the slightest idea whether he knows what he's talking about or not. Blasting? Wow! But you give faith and trust when you give love. 'He can do it,' she added.

The old man stood in the atrium with hands on hips and laughed at the pair of them. 'I don't know when I've had so much fun,' he chortled. 'You two are Hansel and Gretel, wandering through the woods, did you know that?'

'More clichés!' moaned John. 'Tell you what, Marcie—you lay on a meal for tonight, and I'll split down to Star Lake and pick up the necessaries. We'll have the deluge re-routed by tomorrow, for sure.'

'Ring the firebell and everything runs out your ears,' his grandfather snorted. 'You need a blasting permit. What the devil kind of a lawyer are you?'

'So all right,' his grandson returned, 'I need a permit, I'll *get* a permit. And if you're trying to rub it in that I'm a corporate lawyer, I'll switch the whole firm to criminal law. How about that?'

'The trouble with your father's generation was Perry Mason,' the old man told him. 'And I don't know a quicker way to starve to death than to make such a switch. But I won't fight it—go ahead, Lone Ranger. I'll be glad for a couple of hours of quiet here with the most beautiful girl in the country.'

'Watch out for this wolf,' John instructed her as he started for the front door.

'Oh, I will,' she murmured. 'Flattery will get him everywhere.'

'Hey, you're my girl, woman! Don't you forget it.'

'I don't remember any strings tied on me,' Marcie told him pertly. 'Why should I take second-hand charm when I can go straight to the source?'

'I'll hurry,' he threatened, and ran, laughing, out into the sunshine.

'And now,' she insisted, turning to the old man, 'you're going to sit right down here and tell me about my mother.' Which took up most of the rest of the afternoon.

'I've got everything,' he reported happily three hours later. 'Dynamite, permit, advice, everything.' He looked years younger than she knew him to be. Boyish, filled with an enthusiasm that gleamed in his eyes and was reflected by his whole rugged face. How

could *any* girl not fall in love with him? she asked
herself. As her hands busied themselves with the
simple supper, she had to struggle to avoid staring at
him. Her own thoughts bugged her. How dared he let
any woman fall in love with him! The nerve of that
man! If I'm his girl, then he's my man, and he'd better
know from the start that I don't share!

'What's that?' John asked from just over her
shoulder. Marcie started, and almost dropped the
frying pan. 'An old family recipe?'

'Oh, surely,' she returned. 'My grandmother's
favourite. It's called—er—I forget.' Which wasn't
exactly a lie. The conglomeration was something she
was making up as she went along. Her eye had been
caught, during her last shopping expedition, by
packets of unleavened bread in the supermarket, the
kind called pitta bread in the Middle East, or way-
bread in the Crusader lexicon. It was made for
families making long trips in the desert—two circular
slabs of bread, fried together lightly, to make an
envelope. And in the pan she was frying little slivers of
lamb, onions, and tomatoes to stuff in the bread
envelopes. Lacking the spices of a typical Lebanese
kitchen, she surreptitiously added four spoonfuls of
mild Mexican Salsa sauce.

'Your grandfather,' she whispered to John. 'He can
eat spicy food?'

'Loves it. What are you up to?'

'Wait and see,' she laughed.

She was so happy as she stuffed the bread that she
hummed a little tune, and the mood carried over into
the meal, after each of these hulking men had had
three helpings and Gramps looked as if he might want

more. She apologised.

'I just don't know how to gauge male appetites,' she offered. 'I hope you're not starving?'

'No indeed.' Gramps and his courtly manners! He knew just what to say and how to say it. Dressed in an open-neck shirt and a light grey suit, he was the epitome of landed aristocracy, she thought. 'You should always get up from a meal leaving a little space for surprises.' She flashed him her best smile. He reciprocated.

John was still struggling. He had elected to pick up the packet, rather than use knife and fork, and the juices were dripping out of one corner and running down his wrist. It looked out of place compared to his grandfather, but it *was* the proper way to eat way-bread, as Marcie knew. Just to emphasise the point, she had knife-and-forked her way through the first half of her meal, then picked up the second half. Show support for your man, that's what Miriam would say. The idea brought on giggles, and she almost choked on the last bite.

'I knew there was something funny going on when my grandson turned out to be such a good cook,' the old man mused. 'And now the secret is unveiled! You know, if I were forty years younger I'd make a play for this young lady. She's too handy to be left out of the family.' He shot a querying look at John.

'Cut it out, Gramps. There are too many match-makers in this family already. Now, for tomorrow——'

Marcie felt a quiver. Before her face could give her away she stomped off to the kitchen and started the coffee water. I can't even understand myself, she thought, as she leaned over the sink and rinsed the mugs out. First he says I'm his girl, then he backs away—too many matchmakers. He wants to ask me something. Good lord, what? Maybe it's not what I thought at all. Maybe he's another one of those fly-by-night characters. Maybe he *wants* some round-heeled broad! I haven't heard him say a word about 'marriage' and 'happily ever after'. Have I been presuming too much? Her wonderful supper was beginning to taste very vile indeed. While her mind wrestled with the thought her hand automatically reached for the antacid pills.

She piled the mugs up on the tray, loaded the hot water into a jug, found the jar of instant coffee, and made for the living room.

'What you need is an electric percolator,' Gramps told her, after his second sip. 'Not that this isn't good coffee, mind you——'

'What this place needs is some electricity,' John amended. 'Maybe when everything's settled we'll get one of those windmill generators. According to the reports, they provide plenty of electricity, even on calm days.'

And there it is again, Marcie thought. 'We'll get', as if there were things he and I would do here. Because he certainly can't be planning to put up a windmill down at the foot of the mountain. Or maybe he and somebody else? She might have carried on the logic, but there was a motor noise.

'Someone's in a hurry,' his grandfather commented. The brakes squealed on the car outside; it sounded almost as if the nose of the vehicle had been thrust through the front door. John got up and strolled towards the door. It's my house, Marcie thought, as she dashed out in front of him and turned the knob—and immediately wished she hadn't.

'I told you there was something strange about this woman!' Beth Fortin crowded in, brushing Marcie aside. She was waving a folded newspaper in her hand. The little blonde was actually dishevelled. Her cheeks were flushed with anger; her eyes sparked danger signals. She took John's arm with her free hand and led him back to the atrium.

'Gramps,' she said in an artificial tone, 'I didn't expect to find you up here.'

'Circumstances change,' the old man said softly. It was only his body that was old, not his brain. There was trouble brewing in the wind, trouble that he meant to stamp out, given the slightest chance. For the moment he waited quietly, and watched.

'So how did you know either of us was up here?' John, in the hunting mode. His voice was entirely normal, but Marcie could see that glint in his eye, and knew it for what it was. See, she told herself childishly, I do know things about him, even though it's only been—well, a month, almost.

Elizabeth Fortin fumbled for the right words, caught off guard by the reaction of the two men. She glared once at Marcie, who was startled at the pure venom of it all. She really hates me, she thought. Why?

'I—er—I went down to the house,' prattled Beth. 'What a terrible mess. Something that *she* did, I suppose?'

'She has a name, Beth. You might try using it.'

'Oh, Gramps!' The little blonde went over and threw her arms around the old man's neck. 'I couldn't—I just couldn't! And neither could you, after you hear.'

'Been investigating, have you?' John enquired. Still casual, that tone—non-committal.

'And it's about time somebody in this family did,' Beth snapped. The atmosphere was getting to her, penetrating the cracks in her armour, leaving little wounds in her soul. 'God only knows what her real name is, but it's certainly not Waters. Look at this!'

'This' was the front page of the *New York Times*, dated two months earlier. It showed a picture of Marcie, laughing, looking down into the face of the Mayor of New York. The small headline said, 'New York Girl a Heroine, Say Fellow Passengers.'

'And look at the name under the picture,' Beth added triumphantly. 'Habib, it says—not Waters!'

John came over behind Beth's shoulder, and seemed to be reading the story associated with the picture. His grandfather took one quick look, smiled, and looked away.

'So why would she be up here under a false name?' The blonde's voice had risen steadily until it became a shriek. 'She's up to no good, let me tell you. And I know what!'

'Do you really?' John said softly. 'Let me see that paper.'

'I knew I'd seen her before,' Beth continued. 'I knew it the moment I saw her. And there she is—right out in public, on the front page of the newspaper.'

'This reads like a marvellous story, Marcie,' Grandfather Harley said quietly. 'You're a real heroine, aren't you? I read something about that hijacking, and——'

'So why is she using a false name?' demanded Beth.

'I——' So far Marcie hadn't been able to see straight. She was being attacked, and out of a clear blue sky, but could see neither the reason nor the need for it. It was all easily explained, but I'm darned if I explain anything to this crazy woman, she told herself. Her lips went rigid. Beside her, John was watching her face. He chuckled at what he saw.

'You were saying you knew why all this, Beth?'

'I certainly do, John. You and Gramps—being men—really have no idea what's going on. I can't blame you. It's all an act, you know. Sweet wholesome Marcie. Somehow or another she wormed her way in with that old fool Vanderpol.'

'Ah. Perhaps he's in it with her? There's a great deal of money involved.'

'Now you're seeing things clearly, John. Thank God you've come to your senses. But it isn't just the money, you know.'

No, Marcie thought desperately, it isn't the money—or anything else. But it *is* a test. For it to be love there has to be faith and trust. And if he doesn't trust me, I might as well know it early. So I'll just sit here like a bump on a log. If he trusts me—well, we'll see. And if he doesn't? the voice of her subconscious mind asked. And if he doesn't, she thought bravely, I'll—I'll go cry a lot, and then go home where I belong. And cry some more? That nagging subconscious again. And cry some more, she agreed. For a long, long time.

She was trying to look composed, which was difficult. Her fists were clenched so tightly that the fingernails were cutting into her palms. She forced an uninterested expression on to her face, although, behind the mask, her nerves were jumping, her mind tense, her ears tuned for every nuance. If he loves me——

'So what else is she trying to do?' John again, prodding, while his grandfather seemed to have found a tremendous interest in the beams of the atrium ceiling.

'I'll show you!' snapped Beth. She walked over to the corner where Marcie's stack of canvases rested, and thumbed through them, starting at the back. 'Ah, here it is.' The woman pulled out the canvas Marcie had been working on during her first week on the mountain. The all-but-forgotten cover illustration for the romance novel, filed away. 'Here, take a good look.'

Beth slammed the canvas down on the easel. The light was fading, but not yet gone. As if to emphasise her point, the blonde moved a kerosene lantern closer and lit it. John and his grandfather both got up, walked over, and stood in front of the picture. Oh, my God, Marcie thought, I *had* forgotten. There are only six more days to the deadline, and the painting is—— How in the world did John's face get on that? He has cause for complaint! What in the devil could I say now?

'You see it?' grated Beth. 'A terrible picture for a sleazy book! She means to make you the laughing stock of the whole country, John. For some reason the little bitch has decided to poison you with a shot of her special venom!'

The two men continued their assessment. Behind them Marcie was beginning to feel suffocated. There had to be some limit to Beth's imagination, but she painted a plausible picture. Plausible, but untrue. And I don't intend to say a word, she told herself sternly. He either trusts me, or he doesn't. But her stomach was not in agreement with her mind. It roiled and boiled, and there was a bitter taste in her mouth. Maybe I should just go, she thought. Never mind packing, just get up and go. Her hands unfolded and reached for the arms of her chair—then stopped in mid-air. John was staring at her.

There was a message being transmitted, but not on her frequency. She just could not understand, but her hands returned to her lap, and she settled back into the chair, more deeply than before.

'Well.' Grandfather Harley, settling back in his chair, toying with the knife-edge crease in his immaculate grey slacks.

'Yes.' John, doing the same. Both of them staring at Beth, left standing at the easel alone, and feeling the pressure bearing down on her. Like Marcie, Beth had cast her entire future on this one turn of the dice, and was almost cracking. She was dressed as closely to men's attire as one could get: grey skirt, grey jacket and tie, a plain and simple white blouse, with no feminine condescension. And her tie was bothering her. Her fingers plucked at it nervously, loosening it, twisting at it.

'Yes, well——' John began. The sound of his voice crackled through the silence and seemed to break it up. His grandfather cleared his throat. Marcie shifted in her chair. It's the eleventh hour, she told herself. The jury has heard the evidence, and has arrived at a decision. I'm not sure that I want to hear it.

'First of all, I knew all about Marcie's name,' John

said solemnly. 'You're not the only one with access to a clipping service, Beth. Her baptismal name is Waters. She changed it to Habib by deed poll after she was adopted by the Habib family. Nothing wrong with that. And the newspapers, of course, have made her well known. It took a lot of guts to do what she did. I'm proud to be able to say I know a woman like that. Proud.'

His grandfather cleared his throat again.

'As for the picture,' John continued, 'I think it's sort of cute. And recalling that romance novels are the largest sellers in the United States, I think the only way I could get as much attention would be to pose for a *Playgirl* centrefold—and I'm not quite up to that. When this book comes out, Beth, I recommend you get a copy, and preserve the cover. It might turn out to be a collector's item.'

'John?' Beth seemed to be having ear trouble. 'You can't mean any of this, John! You can't. You're a sensible corporation lawyer, with a great future staring you in the face. It will all be gone if any of your clients——'

'Save your breath, Beth.' John stood up and took the blonde by the arm. 'Let me tell you something else. If everything you told me tonight had been a complete surprise to me, I would still have believed in Marcie. Love does that to a man. Now, if you people will excuse us, I think I'll just escort Beth out to her car and make sure she gets off the mountain.'

'My God,' stammered Marcie, watching the pair of them disappear down the hall. 'He—I——'

'Yes,' his grandfather laughed, 'the boy surprises me from time to time. He did that with a great deal of panache, didn't he?' The old man stood up and opened his arms. Marcie bounced out of her chair and was crying on his shirt-front when John came back into the room.

'Gramps!' he scolded as he came in. 'Can't anybody get the message? That's *my* girl you're hugging!' He sounded aggrieved. Marcie managed to clear one eye to look. There was a wide grin on his face. Before she could think, her wildly disobedient body whirled her out of the old man's arms and into those of his grandson. 'Now that's more like it,' John murmured into her hair. 'You sure do cry a lot, don't you, love? Why now?'

'Because I'm so happy,' she sobbed.

'And this morning?'

'Because I was so mad at you!'

'And a few days ago, down at the cottage?'

'Because—because I was so miserable.'

'A universal pancacea, I suppose?'

'I don't know what that means. I'm not a lawyer.'

'I suspect I'm not either,' he sighed. His grandfather seemed to have disappeared somewhere. John led her over to the divan and pulled her down on his knees. 'Now, how about Friday?'

'Friday?' The change of subject had gone by Marcie too quickly. She fumbled for an answer.

'Yes. How about if we get married on Friday?'

'I—married?' she stuttered. 'I—— What about your mother?' Almost a whisper now, with a frightened look on her face.

'My mother lives in solitary splendour at Hanapepe, Hawaii. I fly out to see her twice a year.'

'But she could never accept me. Not as a—— Not as your wife.'

'She'll accept,' John said grimly, 'or she'll be a lot more solitary than she is. There's no reason for you and I to waste our lives because of her ancient prejudices. So how about it? We'll get married on Friday.'

That's not fair, Marcie protested to herself. How can I get married on Friday? I have to tell Miriam and Hafez, and they have to meet John, and then— Miriam would kill me if we don't have a church wedding, and orange blossom and music and a white dress with a veil, and——

'I can't,' she returned sadly. Out in the kitchen a glass crashed on to the floor. John looked as if someone had just kicked him in the solar plexus. A very large silence settled over the house—so much silence that Marcie could hear the tiny squeak of the propane refrigerator going about its appointed business.

'You can't?' John, in a tone that Pharaoh might have used as he watched the Israelites crossing the Red Sea in front of his invincible army. He shook his head, as if clearing an obstruction in his ears. The kitchen door swung open, and his grandfather came back into the room. Silence again.

'What a terrible trial lawyer you are!' the old man chided. 'That was two questions you asked her, not one. Can't you get anything right?'

'Mind your own damn business!' John snapped at him. 'You mean——' He stopped talking and stared at the tiny frightened face resting on his shoulder. What have I done now? Marcie screamed at herself. What have I done?

John cleared his throat. It must be catching, Marcie thought. She sat up straight. If my ship is going to sink, she decided, I'll go down with my colours flying. Fire away, John Harley. You don't scare me—not much you don't. Then how come I'm shaking all over?

'Marcie Waters Habib,' he started off very slowly, very distinctly, 'I love you.'

That seemed clear enough. Marcie nodded in agreement. 'I love you, too,' she returned. He seemed to have started breathing again.

'Marcie Waters Habib,' he stated. 'Will you marry me?'

'I—well—yes,' she managed. 'But you——'

'One answer at a time!' He held up a stop-sign hand. In the background his grandfather chuckled, and wandered off. There were not going to be any other questions—not immediately, that was. John snatched Marcie up close to him, moulding her soft curves into his hard frame, and those lips took control of her as before. Some ten minutes later, thoroughly out of breath, he pushed her back slightly, and brushed the hair off her perspiring forehead. But not all that far, she reminded herself. His wandering hand returned to the curve of her breast, teasing her through her thin shirt.

'Now then, Marcie. Will you marry me on Friday?'

'No,' she gasped, 'I can't do that. It's not possible. First, you have to ask Hafez——'

'Who?'

'Hafez—my father.'

'Oh yes. For an orphan you have a pile of relatives, kid.'

'I—yes. My adopted family is big. You have to ask Hafez.'

'Isn't that a little old-fashioned?' he queried.

'Yes, and then Miriam has to look you over. And the boys have to meet you. And then —— For twenty years Miriam has been planning on my wedding, and——'

'And we can't do that by Friday, can we?' She looked up at him again, searching for trouble. And found only laughter.

'No,' she sighed. 'We can't possibly do that by Friday. Would you mind terribly wearing a morning suit?'

'No, I wouldn't mind,' he laughed. 'Of course you realise I'd have to rent one. Not even Grandfather owns one of them. But what happens if Hafez turns me down?'

'He wouldn't dare,' she giggled. 'Miriam wouldn't let him. Suitors don't grow on trees out in Cambria Heights.'

'Well, thank God for Miriam,' sighed John. 'What do I call her?'

'What I do,' she chuckled. 'When she's angry I call her Ma'am. Other times I call her Mother. You should, too. I'll teach you how to say it in Arabic. It has a lovely flavour.'

'So do you,' he sighed, and went about taking another sample or two.

The next morning they had a late breakfast. 'We may have to go back to the City earlier than I expected,

Gramps,' said John. 'These scrambled eggs are delicious, Marcie. What's in them?'

'A secret recipe,' she laughed. 'Drink your coffee. I'm not giving away any more secrets until after the wedding.'

'So there's to be a wedding?' Grandfather Harley beamed at them both. 'I said it when I first met you, Marcie. You could have been my granddaughter, and now you will be!'

'Don't count your chickens,' his grandson managed around a mouthful of bacon. 'I still have to ask Hafez.'

'Of course,' the old man agreed. 'It's the only way.'

'You don't even know who Hafez is!' And they're at it again, Marcie sighed. I'd better retire to a neutral corner.

'Of course I know,' laughed Gramps. 'I'm a good lawyer. I listen at keyholes.'

'Gramps! You were spying on us?'

'Only for a little while, boy. Your track record has been terrible, I just thought to make sure you were on the right course. This sausage is good too, Marcie,' Gramps added. 'After the marriage, could I drop in from time to time and get a decent meal?'

'Of course, you old fraud,' chuckled Marcie. 'You—— Oh, Gramps, if only you were fifty years younger!' She came around the table, knelt at his side, and hugged him.

'See what I told you, boy? You're lucky that I'm too old for the competition. You wouldn't have stood a chance in *my* day!'

The old man refused to go out with them. 'Got to get that spring under control,' John said. He took Marcie by the hand and the pair of them raced out into the sunshine and, laughing, got to work.

John's truck had a winch on the front. It was child's play to pull her jeep out of the water and off to one side. 'Let it dry out in the sun,' he told her. It was an order, plain and simple, and Marcie found that her old urge to make a fuss had disappeared. It *was* an order. But when they were working side by side she had given him one or two orders, and he had made no protest. And that proves something, she thought. We can share—we *will* share. He's my best friend, and I have to learn to be his. It can't be impossible!

With renewed faith she joined him as he puzzled around the bulldozer.

'It's the blade,' he said. 'We can't get it up because the engine is soaked. And we can't pull it forward because the blade digs in.'

'So we pull it backward,' she suggested hesitantly, looking out to where the back end of the vehicle was almost under water.

'So we pull it backward,' he agreed. 'One of us will swim out there and put the cable on that back towing pintle.'

'One of us?' More hesitant than before. The water was still shooting up a maelstrom in the middle of the pool and she had too many unpleasant memories about her own recent swimming exploits.

'Yes,' laughed John. 'Me. You just sit here in the truck, and see that nobody steals it.'

'I guess I could do that,' she said. 'Did you really like my cover picture?'

'No,' he said. 'Did you really outface those hijackers?'

'I told you the whole story last night,' she said

firmly. 'I was going to tell you sooner, but——'

'But you wanted to see if you could trust me, didn't you?'

'I—yes. In all the time we've known each other you had never said——'

'Said what?'

'That you loved me.'

'Well, I do. And I love your cover picture. My wife is going to make me famous. I'll have all the women in New York hanging around my office!'

'I don't think I'll mail it,' sighed Marcie. 'I think I'll burn it on the bonfire. Hadn't you better start swimming?'

The grin was back on his face again, broad and comforting. 'I've got a terrible ego, Marcie. You'll have to pamper it for a time until I learn better.'

'I will,' she told him, putting her hands up on each of his cheeks. 'People have to work to make a marriage go, John. That's what Miriam always told me. And I plan to. Now go hook up that tow-line. Your grandfather is eager to be away.'

He kissed her nose, picked up the heavy hook and line, and waded into the pool. God must have been paying special attention to that section of the Adirondacks at just that moment, for the bulldozer came out of the water as easily as if it had been designed for underwater work. They towed it over to the other side of the clearing to sit and wait beside the jeep.

'And now for the *pièce de résistance*,' said John. 'you stay here, Marcie. I don't expect any trouble, but just in case.'

'Now it's dynamite time? That scares me.'

'No need to,' he returned. 'The plan is simple, and I've had the training. But you just stay here, because there's always one time in a thousand that things seem to go wrong. Right?'

She acknowledged, but her heart wasn't in it. As she watched him trudging back up to the pool, his grandfather came out on the porch, shading his eyes against the morning sun. John's figure disappeared on the far side of the pool, and there was an endless wait. The old man waved to her, and sat down in the rocking chair on the porch. Marcie shifted her weight in the seat. The sun was getting at the vinyl seat covering, warming it up. She was wearing her shorts, and things were getting a little uncomfortable where the material ended and her bare legs began. She nibbled at her fingertips—an old childhood habit. Miriam had finally resorted to putting mustard on her childish fingertips, but that cure had only lasted for a month or two. Strange, she told herself, how those long-distant scenes are coming back to mind. Because I'm worried?

It was time to stop worrying. John was coming around the side of the pool area, dragging a little wire-dispenser in his hand, and laying a trail of contact wire behind him. Marcie jumped up in the seat and offered him a hero's welcome.

'Well, I haven't done anything yet,' he laughed, 'but I'll take the reward anyway.' The kiss flustered her. She couldn't quite see why the dynamite hadn't exploded from it all.

'Stick to business!' his grandfather called from his seat on the porch. John waved to him, pulled out the detonator box, and began to screw the wires on to the electrical connections.

'Everything's set now,' he reported at last. 'The dynamite is set under the outside lip of that rock. When I push in this plunger it will generate a little surge of electricity, just enough to explode the cap on the dynamite sticks. And then, varoooooom! and all our troubles will be over.'

'It won't—— Nothing else? It won't blow things all over?'

'Not a chance. That's solid granite. Trust me.' And since she did, there was no further problem—at least not in her mind. John looked all around the area carefully. 'Don't want to catch some deer in the wrong place,' he told her.

'Nor my bear,' she said. 'She really did have cubs. They've come up the mountain a couple of times.' There was a wistful sound in her words, and he caught it.

'I hope you like children, Marcie,' he said casually, looking over at his grandfather.

'Oh, I do,' she said, trying to be equally casual about it. To emphasise her position, she scanned the lower side of the mountain.

'Well, that's nice,' said John, but the casual tone was gone. 'I've always wanted a family, Marcie. How about one boy and one girl?'

'You can't order them that way,' she giggled. 'But if it doesn't come out right, we could keep trying?'

His hand came over on top of hers and patted it gently. 'Now,' he said, 'I'm the king of the hill. Let it go, baby!' His right hand twisted and pushed down.

There was a second or two of delay, and suddenly all hell broke loose.

The dynamite exploded, the big rock split into a million pieces and went splattering all over the landscape. There was a crash from the inside of the house, and dust blew in a wide cloud under the hand of the north wind.

When the dust cleared and silence was restored, John and Marcie stood side by side at the truck, disbelieving. 'Oh my,' she offered. He shook himself, and brushed ineffectively at the dust settling all over him. From up at the pool they could hear liquid running, and in moments a small rainbow formed over the old watercourse. 'Well,' he said.

Not knowing what else to say, she started to brush him off.

'We're starting our married life with a big bang,' he punned mercilessly.

'It was a very *good* explosion,' she told him firmly. 'You do a wonderful job!'

'So do you,' he laughed, swinging around to sweep her up in his arms. She clung tightly as he carried her up towards the house. 'I can't believe how lucky I am, love.'

'Because of the explosion?' Marcie snuggled closer, fitting her head against his shoulder.

'Because of you, silly. Because of you. Is Hafez a very big guy?'

'No,' she giggled. 'I'm bigger than he is. You're not scared?'

'Petrified,' he laughed. 'Where did Gramps go?'

'I'm right here.' The old man came out of the house wearing a massive grin. Ear to ear, and maybe farther.

In his hand he held a five-pound rock. He held it up.

'Oh, my!' Marcie managed.

'The atrium?' John queried.

'Right through the centre,' his grandfather laughed. 'Bullseye! You fixed the plumbing, but now you need a new roof. Why don't we stop off in Lake Placid and get a contractor to come up here?'

'That sounds like a good idea,' Marcie squeezed in. Her future husband looked down at her solemnly, then produced a grin to match his grandfather's.

'I told you one in a thousand have this problem,' he chuckled. 'And I suppose you've got a cliché to fit, Gramps?'

'I'm not sure,' the old man returned. 'How about, *people who live in glasshouses shouldn't blast stones?*'

The trio stood smiling at each other, none being willing to be the first to laugh. Marcie nestled closer to John, pulling his hands around her and clasping them at her waist. 'It's going to be fun, married into this family,' she said. John pulled her back against his stomach, and one of his fingers tickled her just below the ribcage.

'I've got to check my suitcase,' said Grandfather Harley. He turned away and headed for the house. Then, over his shoulder, 'There's something in there I've got to get my hands on.'

'Me too,' John murmured in Marcie's ear. His hands left their toying at her waist and marched smoothly up to cup her breasts. She tingled as her own hands came up on top of his, holding him locked in possession. She leaned her head back and smiled at him.

'You're a scandalous rascal, John Harley,' she said sweetly, 'and I hope you never change!'

Harlequin Romance

Coming Next Month

2863 BRIDE ON APPROVAL Elizabeth Ashton
Sancia desperately wants to be free from her restrictive upbringing,
yet she can't bring herself to escape by way of an arranged
marriage—not even to the charming Italian count chosen for her!

2864 THE GOOD-TIME GUY Rosemary Badger
Her boss's relentless pursuit causes problems for office manager
Sarah Ames. She's come to Brisbane with her sights fixed on a
career and has no time for a man only interested in playing games!

2865 IMPULSIVE ATTRACTION Diana Hamilton
During their first magical meeting in the moonlit woods, it doesn't
seem to matter that he's a mysterious itinerant sculptor, while
she's a respectable bank manager. But by daylight, the differences
between them threaten to destroy their love.

2866 SLEEPING TIGER Joanna Mansell
There's nothing sensible about social butterfly Lady Sophia's
suddenly inspired decision to follow a teacher to the Sahara so she
can do some worthwhile work with him there. It certainly changes
her life—but not quite in the way she expects....

2867 EXCLUSIVE CONTRACT Dixie McKeone
Against all the professional counseling rules about not getting
romantically involved with a client, Janet Talbot enthusiastically
sets out to rescue an unusually charming housebreaker from a
life of crime!

2868 AN OLD AFFAIR Alexandra Scott
Only her father's urgent need for money sends Arabella seeking
help from the man she had loved and mysteriously lost seven years
ago. His price for giving it is high—one Arabella isn't sure she
wants to pay.

Available in October wherever paperback books are sold, or
through Harlequin Reader Service.

In the U.S.
901 Fuhrmann Blvd.
P.O. Box 1397
Buffalo, N.Y. 14240-1397

In Canada
P.O. Box 603
Fort Erie, Ontario
L2A 5X3

Can you keep a secret?

You can keep this one plus 4 free novels

ATTRACTIVE, SPACE SAVING BOOK RACK

Display your most prized novels on this handsome and sturdy book rack. The hand-rubbed walnut finish will blend into your library decor with quiet elegance, providing a practical organizer for your favorite hard-or soft-covered books.

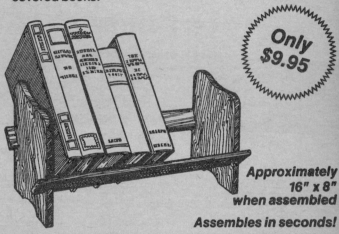

Only $9.95

Approximately 16" x 8" when assembled

Assembles in seconds!

To order, rush your name, address and zip code, along with a check or money order for $10.70* ($9.95 plus 75¢ postage and handling) payable to *Harlequin Reader Service*:

Harlequin Reader Service
Book Rack Offer
901 Fuhrmann Blvd.
P.O. Box 1396
Buffalo, NY 14269-1396

Offer not available in Canada.

*New York and Iowa residents add appropriate sales tax.

BKR-1A

It was a misunderstanding that could cost a young woman her virtue, and a notorious rake his heart.

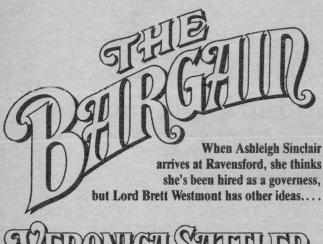

When Ashleigh Sinclair
arrives at Ravensford, she thinks
she's been hired as a governess,
but Lord Brett Westmont has other ideas....

Harlequin Intrigue

In October
Watch for the new look of

Harlequin Intrigue

. . . because romance can be quite an adventure!

Each time, Harlequin Intrigue brings you great stories, mixing a contemporary, sophisticated romance with the surprising twists and turns of a puzzler . . . romance with "something more."

Plus . . .
in next month's publications of Harlequin Intrigue we offer you the chance to win one of four mysterious and exciting weekends. Don't miss the opportunity! Read the October Harlequin Intrigues!